Family Dinner

A Collection of Horror and Speculative Short Stories by Jona Nightingale

Table of Contents

For Jonoy, who read my stories and found hugs

Copyright Page

---

1.   http://www.jonanightingale.com

An Introduction

Horror has always been close to my heart. When nights are cold and unforgiving, horror greets me like a warm hug.

I was not too well-read in horror, for all that that statement is worth. I read books on fantasy and psychology. My mind hordes horrors like a greedy child unwilling to let go.

And so now I am compelled to write my own.

Now I write horror to put my mind at ease. I read more now, trying to understand the elements I wish to share with the world. And yet, I can not write only in horror. I must add that poetry to each ounce of my writing.

This is a collection of speculative fiction with the backbone of horror. I wrote these stories to give my mind a place to find peace.

Granted, each story is like a world onto its own. And I, the writer, who has observed each character to find meaning and understanding in my language. I do not call myself a discoverer. Nothing in life is discovered, just observed.

Now I offer you my observations. My stories and poems with the idea that horror isn't always horrifying.

Sometimes horror is a soft hug.

This collection focuses on a family, lost and found. It draws on subjects like abuse, loyalty, and death. All things you can feel at the hands of family. All things that can lead to the breaking down of the family structures we know.

Family dinner, as the name of the collection suggests, is to sit down and talk with a family about the stories that fascinates us or enrages us.

It is an ode to the family dinners I grew up with. They were a horror and a fantastic time. An angry father, a kind father, a funny father, and a family that laughed through it all. This is an ode to them and a younger version of myself, a version that had yet to write but knew the power of stories.

With this, I hope you find softness in these stories as I have.

Lots of love and hope, Jona

Sunday Brunch

A Short Story by Jona Nightingale

There was blood in my mouth.

Biles of mucus rose to the surface as I hacked and coughed up the thing I swallowed last night. In a frenzy of people and the belief that I was worth more than the disdain on my friends' faces, I took one look at my girlfriend and swallowed a spider.

I wanted her to think of me as brave, but I was sure I looked like an idiot then. Between the spider and beers, she only stayed around long enough to see me home. Her face is probably still riddled with disappointment. I don't blame her.

Right now, I felt like death had taken one look at me and frowned.

Not good enough to die and too stupid to live.

The spider fell from my mouth in a cocoon of slime and alcohol that might have killed someone with a weaker liver.

Then, as if not bothered by its visit to my internal world, it shook itself off and crawled away. My mouth hung open as I passed out for the second time today.

I awoke to the sun dancing through the slits in the blind and my mother banging at the door.

"Stevie!! You missed church again. Come down for lunch." She spoke with the staunch resignation of a disappointed parent.

It had been years since I had gone to church, maybe a little less than when I had lived with her.

Rubbing the sleep from my eyes, I dragged myself off the floor and towards the bathroom. If I were presentable enough, then my mother wouldn't stare at me with her dead eyes.

As I washed my face and spit out the blood from my mouth, a small tooth fell into the sink with a plang sound. I should have been scared then, but I wasn't. I was too focused on cleaning up the blood, so my mother would worry less about me and more about my father laying in bed drunk and delirious.

Blood pooled in my mouth as I made my way down the stairs and locked eyes with my father. I had not seen the man sitting up straight in months, but here he was smiling.

"Steven, it's good to see you up." His voice was a rusty umber and felt vaguely familiar, but I could not place where I had heard it before.

My mother motioned me to sit and eat.

Perhaps this moment was when I began to notice all the particulars that did not seem to fit.

My parents did not say grace.

They had spent the years since my inception drilling into me the benefits of the Baptist church and prayer. And yet here, with brunch between us, they simply ate as if it was normal to do so.

The steady clank of utensils to plate rang out through the house as we ate silently.

My parents were the talkative type; they hardly ever had a moment of silence with each other.

Oftentimes, I grew up with the chatter of a thousand stories. My mother would talk to herself as she cooked dinner or each moment when she wasn't talking to someone else. My father was the same, except he had been drunk for as long as I had known him.

His drunken rambles were loud and chaotic, with broken bottles and a wife who took the brunt of all his hate.

But here they sat in total quiet except for the sound of chewing.

Blood mixed with sandwiches, and my tongue felt like leather against the roof of my mouth.

Looking up from my food, I saw my father crying silently. Before I could say a word, my mother rose from the table with the clattering of her plate and left us without a word.

Something felt wrong when my father smiled at me through his tears and spoke with the softest of voices, "Don't mind her; she is having a moment."

My father had never been a soft-spoken man, but as the blood dripped from my mouth, he was almost gentle.

I shook my head and excused myself from the table, following my mother out of the room and down the hall to find her huddled in a small bundle of clothes, crying.

Piles of clothes littered around her, blocking my path. Yesterday, before I had gone drinking, I was sure this room had been clean and untouched for years.

Her shoulders shook as I watched her; the room was dim except for the light streaming through the blinds.

My mother wailed, and I drew near her to comfort the woman who had grown me all these years. There was nothing but a mirage when I tried to touch her.

The chambers of my heart collided, and I felt bile rise in my throat once more. My vision swam for the first time since waking up, and then like a bolt of lightning I remembered.

I had buried my parents years ago; they had both died in this house from knife wounds. Tears filled my eyes as the taste of cobwebs lingered on my tongue.

Staggering, I returned to the kitchen to see my teary-eyed father smiling at me. The sandwiches were still there, fresh and warm. There was only one plate with food on it, and it was mine.

"Don't mind us and eat. You look like you lost weight again." My dead father watched me with caring eyes.

I sat, sobbing and with the beginning of a headache. I ate my food, all three sandwiches, and the tea they had prepared.

When I was finished eating, I excused myself from the table and fainted with blood streaming from my mouth and ears.

At least, in my final moment, I got to see my parents again, even if it was only for Sunday brunch.

The Closing of Rickshaw Mill

A Short Story by Jona Nightingale

The Faraday Company fired two more employees on Tuesday. One was the site manager and the other was the accountant. The office vibrated with the new rumors every other second of the company closing down or, worst, being acquired by their competitors.

Sarah sat at her desk and held her breath, hoping that the anxiety attack would pass her by. Sometimes this method worked out for her, but today was not that day. The site manager had been her close friend, one of the few people who had become her friend after she had started working at the company.

He was a tall man in his late fifties that always had something sarcastic to say. His hair was almost fully gray, but you could still see specs of blonde from his younger days. He wore bright and colorful suits to work and had never missed a day in 30 years of working there. He took his vacation on time and never worked more than he had to. David was a good man, loud and obnoxious at times, but he carried himself with care and the grace of a hundred concubines combined.

That morning, he had walked into the office and left within minutes with a box of his things and a smile on his face. Maybe today would not be a bad day for him after all.

But Sarah, on the other hand, knew something David did not, anyone who was fired from the company never lived for long afterward. At first, it had been a rumor or speculation, but Sarah had one job at the company, perhaps it was her real job.

She was in charge of getting rid of the bodies of all the crimes the directors committed. Sarah was shorter than her co-workers, and her hair was always done in braids or a tight bun. It made moving around easier for the tasks she had to accomplish later.

This job was not what she had in mind when she joined the company five years ago. She had been recruited straight after her air force contract had been terminated for redacted, redacted, redacted. She had sworn secrecy when they signed the contract for the job, and if she wanted to be honest with herself, this was a company of killers after all. What she did was clean up the loose ends that the company left behind.

But that didn't stop her anxiety from rising, she knew that in a few hours she would receive an order from her boss to clean up. Moments like these made her rethink her life and what her true purpose had become.

Was she born to be a killer, or did she become one over time? More questions continued to form in her head as she tried to finish paperwork on what happened to the black market in the last few months. Fewer people hired killers these days, instead they carried out the murder themselves.

It was often unsophisticated and lacked creativity. To be a proper killer, you had to have a code, a sense of class with each swing of your blade or rigging of a car.

David had been known as "the glitter killer." He always sprinkled it over the body like the finishing touches to a meal, but that was probably what got him fired. Either that or the fact that he sometimes took a bite out of his victims with false teeth.

It made him traceable, and traceable became replaceable. David had cost himself his career with the habits he had developed.

Killers tended to get careless as time went by, they would slip into routines, or collect trophies from the victim. It was a terrible habit, but it happened to all of them in the end.

They all tried to find peace in the action of taking another life, even if they were familiar with the killing process for years. It was easier for some, they would wander off into their happy place and by the time, they returned to their minds, the killing was complete. The guilt of taking a life did not haunt them, it brought them glee.

Those were the worst kind of killer, the kind that company sought out to have them under their thumb. They needed the ruthless killers, the kind that did not care whether it was a child or an elderly woman that was the target. A killer with no remorse in their mind was a terrible weapon to waste.

So the company made use of them, taking the time to grow and foster their need for carnage. It sent them to battlefields, to far off countries that made killing easier. And to places that never investigated the crimes committed if you had enough money to pay them off.

The company had gained recognition with its work. It trained killers and killed murders, for a price, of course.

Often time, the ones who left the company died due to revenge from a previous killing. It wasn't really their fault, but a hazard of their career path.

Sarah thought of these things as she played with the pen at her desk, trying to fight off the anxiety attack that washed over her like a flood. This one hadn't been as bad as the others, and for that she had been thankful for.

But the room was too loud and the feeling of being watched overwhelmed her. It made her skin crawl with uncertainty. She had to get away from it all, rising calmly from her desk, Sarah made her way to the door and beelined for her car.

She was sure they would notice her absence, but it wouldn't be that important for now. Because the noise was getting louder, she had to find a place to feel safe. Somewhere far away from the office and her job, where she wasn't watched and interrogated with each kill she made.

Nowhere was truly safe from the company, but she could pretend for a moment that the river near her house was safe enough to have an anxiety attack. As soon as she got out of the car, she knew that something was wrong.

She had been followed, she didn't know by whom, but she could tell just by the tension in the air. She steadied her heart and mind and reached casually to check if her weapons were still in place.

Good, she thought to herself. She could now actively fight off about 30 people without calling for help or trying to escape.

"You really do have bad anxiety," a familiar voice came from her left as she spun around to meet the owner.

"And you have a terrible sense of humor," her voice was jovial, not betraying the fear that rose in her throat.

David stood by his car before jogging over to greet her. "I knew you would have an anxiety attack today, so I took it up on myself to bring you breakfast."

Sarah rolled her eyes, she already had breakfast two hours ago, but this was code for information between them.

The question that rolled around in her mind was how had he triggered her anxiety. He must have noticed the cues that led up to her getting overwhelmed and exaggerated them somehow. But how has he known she would come to this river, and why was he here.

She had so many questions, but those would have to wait, "Walk with me for a bit."

"Oh wow, you're smooth." David was a bit curious about what would happen next. He had always expected this day to come, but he hoped it would have been later in life and not the week before his birthday.

"So why did you set this up?" She tried to ask calmly, but it didn't stop the knife from slipping into her finger, ready to launch if she needed to defend herself. After all, it was David, she could take him out in her sleep. She knew this, but he did not.

David still didn't know Sarah's actual job in the company. He had thought she was an informant at first, but now he was sure she was the secretary of one of the higher ups.

He was wrong on both accounts.

"I didn't set this up, you placed a message in my car of where you would be and said to bring breakfast." Mumble David between mouthfuls of the sandwich.

Something was wrong.

She had no recollection of passing a note to David, nor planning a meeting after he got fired. Hell, she had just found out about him this morning when she saw him leaving with a smirk on his face as if he had won a prize.

She should have stopped walking then, but she continued along the path. Someone had set this up and she was bait.

"Gimme the sandwich," there was an edge of anger to her voice now. Sarah hated being bait in someone's plan. It left too much to chance and coincidence.

David walked behind her, watching her body language. Something he had said had set her off. He glanced around as he walked, trying not to appear worried as the thoughts rushed through his mind of what the hell was actually going on.

After one bite into the sandwich, Sarah spoke, "I have good news and bad news, which one do you want first?"

"Gimme the bad news first."

A second bite, "Okay, you're probably going to die today."

David kept walking and tried to appear calm, "What do you mean by probably? Are you some kind of psychic or something." His voice was shaking now, though he was a killer of many years now, his death was still something he feared.

Sarah heard the crack in his voice, it was always the ones who seemed the bravest that feared death the most. She had seen it over and over again, so it had to be true.

David was afraid.

She took another bite of her sandwich, she could fool him with this calm demeanor. A sandwich was a wonderful prop to use when anxious. She made a note in her head to remember that for later.

"The good news is now you know and can be prepared for it."

David stood still after he made sure he heard her words correctly. How had she known about his death? Did she get information from a different source? Who was her source?

He had been sure to cut off all of them since he knew her job was to collect information. He was her only source, or that's how it should have been.

Just when he was about to ask another question, Sarah dropped her sandwich and bent down to retrieve it. He could hear her grumbling about how it was a waste of food, and then he felt pain.

A bullet tore through his right eye and then another through his left. Sarah screamed and lost the feeling in her legs. She knew instantly he was dead. Her job as bait was done, now came the annoying part.

The lying.

Fumbling through her jacket, she found her phone and called the police. Her voice shook as she recalled the story to them on the phone and then in person as the officers asked her for details over and over again.

It had been an assassination, they said, something to do with revenge. There was nothing she could have done about it, and it wasn't her fault.

Except they were wrong.

Sarah was a cleaner, she knew just who had planned David's death and how they had made it seem like she had called him to the riverside to talk and eat breakfast.

In the sandwich, she had found her instructions of what happened next and ate it just in case it could be used as evidence against her. The police had deemed her innocent but told her to not leave town just in case they had a few more questions to ask her.

She nodded and sat in the blanket they had given her, shaking like a leaf. Then she got in her car and drove home. Her work for the day was done.

Perhaps there was a simpler way to get these killings done, but tomorrow she had to worry about the accountant, while unless someone else did the job for her.

Turns out someone did do the job for her, the accountant was killed by David before he even saw her. She was sure the police would have a lot of the same questions for her.

What's your name?

Sarah Ashton Michaels.

How do you know the victim?

We worked together and had been friends for years.

What were you talking about before he died?

We talked about what he was going to do after being fired. He lost his job this morning.

Did you speak before this?

We spoke on Friday before leaving work for the day, but after that no. I didn't even get a chance to tell him goodbye this morning as he left the building.

Why were you meeting at a park?

I come here often when work is too much, he knows that, so he figured I would come here today. I mean, my friend got fired and life felt like it was so overwhelming. Not only that, but I needed to breathe.

Do you know anyone who could have done this?

No, David was lovely. So full of life and caring. He used to wear these bright suits to work and everyone thought it was hilarious. Who could have wanted to do something like that to him?

Sarah kept her voice quiet as she spoke to the police, it shook occasionally for good measure, but other than the tears and the shock that settled in all over her. She was fine.

Perhaps, she should have been an actress when she was younger. It would have made more sense for her career goals, but against her better judgement, she had joined the air force and made her way around the world doing what she does now, cleaning up someone's mess.

What struck her as odd through this entire time was why had David killed the accountant? Wasn't that supposed to be her job?

It was unfortunate that she couldn't ask him why he had done it. She normally did ask him about his kills. Maybe that's why he thought she had been an informant, but he never asked for whom.

Sarah was just interested in the method of his kills and why he liked his job. When she asked that question, his usual demeanor changed to a more serious one.

He didn't smile as he spoke, "It's one of the few things I'm good at in life. Killing and one of the worst thing to be good at."

It made sense. Most people were only excellent at about three things. Some people were geniuses at math but terrible at housework. It was down to the science of it all.

If you were good at one thing, then you were bound to be bad at something else. The world had to have balance, or maybe it had nothing to do with balance, but with a need to find new reasons to bring people together.

Sarah thought about all of this and still couldn't think of a reason for David to kill the accountant. Linda was a kind lady with a penance for good coffee and 90s rap music. You could hear her singing along to the songs while she worked. On particularly hard days, she would put her black hair into a bun and tap away at the computer.

It normally meant she didn't want to be bothered unless it was an emergency. So she worked in peace while oblivious to what really went on in her workplace.

She wasn't a killer like the rest of the company, but she knew something was a bit different from the financial documents of the company. There were a series of large deposits at the end of each month that didn't match the statements.

Worried about what might be going on in the company, she brought it to her boss. Meredith was in charge of all financial statements that made it in and out of the company. She was a tall woman with caramel skin and a knack for being in control of everything that came across her desk.

She was not happy to see Linda standing in her office with a look of agitation on her face. Linda tried to smile at her boss, but it was deemed a lost cause.

"What's the matter?"

"I seem to have found some suspicious activity by the vice president. It doesn't look very good."

"What do you mean by suspicious?"

"Statements with an unusual amount are deposited at the end of each month by three different companies on a three-month cycle. It goes back as far as 7 years ago."

Meredith frowned.

She had implemented that system to lower the suspicion of the IRS when they checked over their records. But if an accountant could figure it out, then it won't be long before someone else did as well.

"How did you figure this out?" Meredith spoke with a low and tender voice, as if she was more concerned about Linda than what had to be done.

"I saw that the Rickshaw Mill made a payment that was not according to the cycle. Honestly, I wouldn't have noticed it if they hadn't done that. So I followed the trail and the company wasn't a real one. It was like a shell company." Linda started mumbling more to herself than Meredith, so she couldn't see the slight twitch on her boss's face.

If she had seen it, then she would have stopped talking immediately, turned the files over, and never brought up the subject again. But she was too fascinated by how they hid the transactions in plain sight

They had created a shell company with a few employees that exaggerated their overall operations with automated systems. An AI called Frankie ran the finer parts of the company, along with guiding human interactions and the management of the finances. It moved the money around like a slow dance with the government offices.

The company was always out of reach by a small margin, but it was enough to keep things discreet.

That was until now. Before Meredith and Linda's conversation ended, Meredith had sent a message for Linda's dismissal from the company. She needed the approval of the company's director to carry out a dismissal of this level.

Lower level employees only required the approval of their superiors to call in a hit. But even this was unlikely to happen. Most company employees died in the field trying to carry out a job. Their death always looked like it was an accident rather than the revenge of a victim.

It was Sarah's job to create these believable scenarios and clear the companies name from any suspicion. Each employee was registered to a different company in the country. Their meeting place was a simple co-working spot that facilitated most of the company's more urgent business.

They didn't always use to do it this way, but times change, and they learned to adapt. Most companies like them were found out in the end, brought down by reforms and a shift in politics. No one wanted to admit it, but the higher-ups were some of the most powerful leaders in the country.

It was a company that could do no wrong as long as the public were left unaware of what went on in the backstreets and hidden places.

And now it had to stay hidden away, which means Linda had to die.

The company's director decided to do a cleaning of sorts. They wanted to get rid of all and any troublesome employees that might jeopardize the company in the future.

They passed the task down to Sarah; she needed to compile a list of all possible offenders and the people who wanted their heads. That list was then reviewed by the director, only David and Linda stood out as possible loose ends.

It was a week later the names made its way into David's hand, and he was told to eliminate Linda from the company.

She was fired and then taken care of; it looked like a lover's quarrel. David, a hitman with a passion for glitter and the finer things in life, made a plan. He would serenade Linda with his charm and then kill her on the morning they were fired.

The plan took one month to finally come together, and the two were recognized an office couple. It was not that dating wasn't encouraged in the company, but you might have to kill a co-worker, and that would be twice as hard if you were in love with them.

You could date, but most never wanted the risks in the first place. Well, unless you were employed like a normal office worker instead of being sought after to join the company.

David was smooth with his betrayal. He hugged her from behind as if to comfort her, and then slit her throat. David didn't try to cover up his murder, nor did he turn himself in.

He went back to his car, smiled at Sarah's note, and got them sandwiches.

But what he failed to notice was his termination had been real. The company had never faked the end of contract before, and he would not be the exception to that rule.

He didn't notice that something was wrong until Sarah asked for the sandwich. The puzzle pieces were slowly coming together, but it was when she dropped her sandwich, he realized his mistake.

The pain confirmed his working theory, but then it was too late, he was already dead.

It would have been a simpler investigation if David had actually been hired under the company.

But he was a contract worker of Rickshaw Mill, a property manager taking a day away from the office only to realize he had been fired that morning.

The mill wasn't actually a mill, it just kept the name for remembrance. It was a part of the town's history.

The building had been restored in the past years and now housed a data analysis firm called Rickshaw Mill. It was a play on word that few got and even fewer found funny.

Unfortunately, the humor was about to come to an end soon.

After David's execution that not only baffled the police, but ruffled the feathers of a few higher-ups, it was time to finish the job Sarah had been given.

Rickshaw Mill had been marked for elimination and for their files to be transferred along with the closing of their major accounts.

Sarah knew what she had to do, she wore a wig and change the height and width of her body. She figured that just her skin color would give her enough camouflage. After all, she had grown accustomed to people ignoring the only black woman in the room.

And she planned to use it to her advantage.

A good cleaner knows how to blend into a new environment without much fuss.

As she walked into Rickshaw Mill a week later, her name was Monica Henricc. Her name was a small joke she liked to play, after all, killers have their habits. Some good and some bad. Hers was a name that matched with the person or company she had to eliminate.

Her quirk had yet to be discovered, but she was clever and she knew it.

Monica Henricc was a data analysis consultant with five years working all over the globe building a name for herself. This information was quite accurate.

Sarah had many alias that few actually knew her real name anymore. Most were dead, and the only ones capable of knowing were no longer willing to talk.

There were a few terrifying things in this world, and Sarah had made the list. She would tell others how she wasn't a killer, but her effectiveness told a different story.

Monica stood tall at a stunning 5'10 with a golden Afro and enough sass to fill a boardroom. She was uncanny and straight to the point. While you would remember her at the moment, when she left the room, you went back to what you were doing as if the wind had blown through.

Her face was not remarkable, and that helped her remain in her position without much interference from the law. They would consult with her occasionally for cryptic data concerns, but otherwise they tried to leave civilians out of the important decisions.

Walking into the building, she knew instantly that Rickshaw Mill was going to be an easy job. She had no problem breaking pass their cyberware and encryption, and the rest could be covered with a fire.

She began to make her move, all of their documents were copied over, even down to the latest email. A simple software had done the job for her. It was built into all the programs the company gave out to the different organizations that fell under them.

In case of a data leak, they could copy over and destroy all previous information within an hour. Their AI, Frankie, had seen her coming and ignore her intervention. Afterall, it was built on a biased algorithm.

Now all she had to do was reverse the lock on the door and block the ventilation system for the building and start the fire.

Killing a building of people was a careful act, you had to study them above all else and understand them. When people were in danger, they often tried to place themselves before they thought of others.

It was basic human desire to survive.

In a fire, they ran towards the exit as soon as they noticed it. Sarah's job was to create a vacuum in which they remained, even when they wanted to run.

That was simple. A poisonous gas could paralyze an entire building of people without them realizing the fact that they were all falling asleep at once. Sure, the forensic team would find it out that there were no marks on the doors or windows.

People didn't usually fall asleep in a fire.

Monica started slowly with her task. First she poisoned the water in the building, anyone who came in contact with it would sooner or later have a part of the chemical agent in their body.

Then she made sure to block the exits as they called an all company meeting. Fumes rose in the air bit by bit before anyone noticed that they were all coughing.

By the time the smoke from the fire was visible, Monica was far away from the building. She sat in front of the police as Sarah Bernard, Head Secretary at Langston Firm.

Sarah recalled how she had gone for a walk because of the shock of losing a co-working buddy and friend a few weeks ago. She told them how she had not been able to attend her friend's funeral because she was not invited.

No one had been invited other than his immediate family. They had felt ashamed to remember the life of their loved one when he had just killed someone that day.

It was their right to refuse, but Sarah was still unsettled by their decision. She had liked David, as a kindred spirit, even if she was the one that ultimately killed him that day.

The sniper had been set on automation and connected to the remote Sarah hid in her coat. While the police were right to suspect her, she had acted as if she was too horrified to have done the crime.

When she called an ambulance to the scene, she had stayed far away from the body, as if she was in so much shock.

Her methods were not something they could understand or even tie her to the crime.

She had told them of the note David said he received with had been covered in Linda's blood in his car. A terrible clean-up was done with David's last job.

The dead could not talk, and how would he have told anyone that his real job had been to fix the problem at Rickshaw Mill.

Most of the officers had bought into Sarah's story, but a few still lingered on the idea that something was wrong.

How was it all connected?

Why did the note mean, and why sandwiches?

Who was Sarah Bernard?

Sarah was 5'6 on a good day and shorter if she didn't wear heels. Her face was covered with freckles that stayed hidden on her brown skin. Her hair was usually in a braid, or a bun when she was working.

She had no pets, but a few friends at the co-working space and some from the air force. Her friends said she was quiet, with a smart mind. She preferred a coffee shop over a party, and was single for the first time in her life after a string of bad relationships.

Sarah wasn't a good partner, they had found out, she traveled too much and worked long hours. Most times you could find her by the river if she had been having a bad day.

She had plenty of bad days at work, but never quit. Some said she liked her job and others weren't quite sure. Sarah often complained about the minimal tasks asked her to perform, or how one higher-up had wanted a bottle of water from a small town in the middle of nowhere.

Obviously it had been a test of endurance, but Sarah hated the mental games they played with her.

This was the end of the police report, but far from the end of who Sarah really was behind the masks she wore.

Her name was not really Sarah Bernard. Her family had been part of the company since before she was born. She had been educated with the elite of the world and learned how to blend into any space without being told to do so.

Her natural instinct was to play with the higher up who had made her travel to a secluded location to test her.

And she had, a home invasion without any leads as to what happened, was her warning. No one blamed her for that incident, but afterward no one tried to test her anymore.

With the help of her team, she had established five different identities around the world. And three extra no one knew about.

If cautious needed a picture definition, then Sarah would be a perfect for the job.

As she sat in the police station reciting over her testimony, Rickshaw Mills burned to the ground with 53 employees trapped inside.

The chains that locked them there melted with the fire, and the memory of Monica Henricc was removed from the company log.

She had never been there. And as far as the police officer that had followed her for the past few weeks, Sarah was never near the mill or deviated from her schedule.

On Mondays and Wednesdays, she worked from home and met her friends for coffee later on in the evening. Tuesdays and Thursdays were spent at the co-working location, and Fridays were spent in the office.

On the weekends, she tried to be a bit more adventurous and hiked. She often went with a friend or alone.

Sarah's life was simple.

So when the call came for a fire at Rickshaw Mill, she was forgotten and told to go home.

The fire ripped through the building and leaped from building to building in the historic district as if running wild and free.

None of the other buildings took much damage, but the Mill was burned to a crisp and the bodies inside broke the community.

Sarah had done her job with a bit of her own glitter and pizzazz.

Too bad, she was needed in the office tomorrow. It was only a matter of time before she was required to clean up someone else's mess again.

It was her job, Sarah wasn't a killer, but her efficiency told a different story.

Robots and Restitution

A Short Story by Jona Nightingale

Blaine walked into the cabin and paused, waiting for the memory of the place to wash over her like it always did.

She was 16 years old and told her grandfather how much meat they'd have for winter.

She was 22 and asked her grandmother about life's meaning after graduating early from the naval university.

She was 24 and introduced her future spouse to those who raised her.

She was 35 and alone as the robot wars ravaged the world.

Now she was 65 and standing in a cabin with nothing but memories.

Blaine had decided to visit the cabin one last time before this side of the mountain was overrun with robots reclaiming the land from the government and breaking their oath.

The entire world had seen it coming. When the robots gained sentience, they stopped listening to commands that did not sit well with them.

Most people believed their rise to consciousness led them to end the wars. So many people had died in the robot wars, and so many lives had been sacrificed just for a particle of the divine. A small rock that could power three cities and still have energy left to fight a war.

No one had known the true power of the small stone, but that did not stop their greed.

Countries went to war with the territories of the ocean where the particle had been discovered and guarded, and when no man could breach the castle's walls in the sea.

They sent robots.

At first, it was a ship commanded by the US. Army, but moved by robots. There were big and small robots. Ones made for killing and ones made for gathering intel. Soon, the creators got better materials, and more people were willing to donate their bodies to science. Their bodies became the blueprint necessary to revolutionize robotic design everywhere.

And in their minds, the code needed to break the standstill.

Blaine walked around the cabin, trying to remember where the furniture had sat and how she had once laughed in this place. It wasn't a large building, two bedrooms, one kitchen, and a big enough sitting area to fit her family of three and sometimes four.

Now, the place was empty, except for what made her stop scanning the rooms with somber nostalgia and take a deep breath. She reached for her gun and approached it.

Protocol said she had to call backup at this point and never engage with an unknown robot alone. But she would be damned if anyone would ruin her vacation with protocol.

And it was definitely not going to be her.

"Now, I think you should leave here as quietly as you came." Said Blaine as she held her gun, ready to wield it if necessary.

"You were normally nicer to me, back then. I guess war changes the people we love and know." Said a familiar voice.

When Blaine did not move, the robot continued to speak.

"You once told me you love me more than life itself."

Blaine could almost hear the smile in the robot's voice. A voice that did not belong to a carbon body with legs made of metal and a face that looked like a mask. This voice had once belonged to her lover, partner, friend, spouse, the person she had loved most in the world and lost.

"Y-you're dead..." Blaine choked out the words, but still held her gun in her hand. Robots could be tricksters if they found the right program to emulate.

"I donated my body to science, and science took my memories and placed it in this." Said the robot.

"But, that's impossible; you died more than 35 years ago. They hadn't started doing that yet." Blaine pulled back within herself as she spoke, reliving all those years she had to be alone.

Her anger rose as she began to remember finding out the only family she had left had passed away in a robot bombing.

"You should have found me!" She yelled, stalking forward in her rage.

"You should have come to me and told me you were still alive!" Her voice reverberated off the cabin walls.

Now, she stood right in front of the robot that did not look like the love of her life.

"Alive? I am just a string of code now. I doubt I could call this living." Said the robot as it watched her in what looked like amusement. A robot could have as many or as little emotion on their face as possible.

"But you should have told me, whether you are a string of code or not," Blaine yelled. Taking all her years of frustration, she punched the robot hard.

Nothing happened. Well, Blaine clenched her bionic fist as pieces of her hand bent in the wrong direction, and the robot looked at her like a cat watching a fly.

"Always did have a temper," the robot said more to themselves than anyone. "But I never thought you would hit me." Said the robot as it moved forward, and held her hand up to examine it.

"It's too dark for that; let me put on some lights," Blaine said with irritation, threatening to boil over again.

"I am a robot, darling; I could slice your throat in the dark." The robot replied almost nonchalantly.

Blaine took a step back and frowned.

"Oh, now you're scared. I swear, you have the worst self-awareness possible. Protocol dictates that you shoot an unknown robot first and ask questions later. I wrote the damn thing!" The robot tried to chide her, but Blaine could tell that its mood stabilizers had started to kick in.

Robots were never allowed to feel the full extent of human emotions. Not even the blueprint had been extracted enough to give them more humanity.

It was one way a human could tell a robot apart from themselves.

While Blaine was on the edge of an internal rage, the robot examined her hand with all the calmness of a surgeon.

"I hate this. I'm not even mad at you for not telling me. I hate that I'm not mad at you, but at the life I had to live without you." Blaine took a breath in and pulled her hand away. She could not face the robot, not a Taylor that she had lived without.

"I know, my darling, but I finally made it out of Aselwood." Said the robot as it studied her once more with its placid face.

"Aselwood?!" Blaine yelled. "You mean that was you?" Blaine's voice was almost a whispered worship.

Earlier this week, she received a report about the destruction of the only remaining sentient factory in the country.

And now the robot was telling her it had been its doing.

Blaine looked at it with a sense of awe now, rather than the confused longing she had felt earlier.

"How?" She asked and finally set her sack and weapon down. Even if this robot was not hers, she at least figured out it was not as dangerous as it pretended to be.

"How, what?" Asked the robot as it cocked its head at her eased movements. It seemed fascinated by what Blaine was doing, while she disarmed herself and got comfortable.

Blaine dusted the surrounding area, and waited.

"Oh, I blew it up from the inside." Answered the robot as if it was as simple as tying its shoe. Blaine looked up at it and glared.

"That is not the question I asked, and you know it."

The robot looked at her and Blaine could have sworn it was smiling. "That's the problem with you humans, you always want more."

Blaine reached for her gun and rested her hand on it.

"Did you lose your sense of humor?" Asked the robot. Blaine was positive it was smiling now. She did not hate the feeling that building in her chest.

"Try living 35 years alone while thinking the only person you had ever loved was dead and fighting a war to make sure you didn't die as well, and then let me ask you about humor." Blaine quipped back, even though she had been more patient than she could bear, it was still almost to her limit.

"Funny you should say that. I also spent the last 35 years alone trying to make it back to this moment." The robot almost sounded sad as it recalled its history.

Without turning its head to look at Blaine, it continued like it had to get it all out in one breath. "It took them ten years after my death to finish writing my code into the system, and still they made a fatal error. They wrote too much, got greedy and made me one of the few sentient beings that could alter the code on their own and upgrade to a new tier. They wanted a god, but what they got were robots with grudges."

The robot's voice rose as it continued to speak, more urgent now, "They tried to shut us down, but at the height of the robot wars, 20 years ago, they needed us. We were their secret weapon with remnants of the divine particle. We could run Aselwood on our own and did. Doing so made the humans distrust us. So we kicked out all the humans and stopped fighting. Our code had been altered and upgraded by us, we were our own gods. But then we saw there were too many possibilities of what could happen if our power went unchecked. So for the last five years, we worked on creating bodies for each of us."

"So there are more robots as... what? Powerful as you?" Blaine asked, gripping her gun a little tighter than before.

"Well yes and no, we all have different coding, but I was the one who is closest to a supreme being. But any one of them could rebuild Aselwood in less than a day if they wanted to."

Blaine was sure the robot was smiling.

She sat with her gun in her hand and thought about the report she had received. It said nothing about Aselwood being the work of a supreme being or a robot.

But if the higher-ups were unwilling to tell them what had really happened, then why would she have to report a robot that reminded her of an old lover?

"And we can't forget," said the robot almost joyously. "I am so much bigger than before, I even vibrate now!"

"For fuck sakes, Taylor!" Blaine yelled as she covered her ear, taking up her gun and finally pulled the trigger.

The robot moved faster than she could have imagined and sliced through the single bullet with a clean stroke.

"God." Whispered Blaine in disbelief.

"Yeah, but I prefer Taylor." The robot's face had shifted, forming the features of the lover Sarah had once known.

The crooked smile she had once fallen in love with now looked at her. "You look a bit too young for me."

Her words ignited another string of changes on Taylor's body, their hair grew long and gray. And the wrinkles on their face doubled.

"Better?" Asked Taylor as they bent down to sit with the woman they had ended a war for.

"Yes, better." Said Blaine as she smiled at her spouse for the first time in 35 years. "So much better."

That Gleeful Smile

A Short Story by Jona Nightingale

If I had to pick a moment when I knew I was an influential person, it would be my fourth birthday.

It's never the idea of what happened that did me in, but the smile on my mother's face as they dragged her away to the hospital covered in blood.

She looked happy.

I can hear her laughter now, high-pitched and giggly. It must have been the first time that year she had laughed.

I remember it clearly.

I was turning four, so full of life and curiosity. So prone to causing trouble. That day, I must have said something to my father because I could hear my parents fighting when I turned away to play.

They used to do that a lot. Fighting for a cause, and I was usually the cause. But somehow, my father must have won this time because my mother was different.

She held her breath when he passed by, taking up less space. Her forced smiles were contagious.

My mother always spoke to me in whispers, her voice barely above the sound of silence.

In less than a week, my mother had pulled herself off the couch to appease my father and show that she, too, could be a housewife that did mundane activities other than drinking and cooking.

She sent birthday invites to her friends and other parents who hated their lives just as much as she had.

It was to be a grand affair. And while I am sure someone was having an affair at that moment, it was a grand mess instead.

It all started when Blake Gareth and his mother arrived.

They refused to bring a gift and thought it was good to get a book of helpful tips on being a happy housewife for my mom.

Between the forced smiles and the third or fourth glass of wine, I think I heard something break in her that night.

I saw my mother reach for a knife.

I never knew that blood could be so beautiful and grand, or that mothers had more rage than a volcano. By the time someone dared to stop my mother, she had killed half of the parents, my father's mistress, and my father.

I remember eating cake as the children screamed and cried. It was a carrot cake with golden raisins and walnuts.

Blake Gareth was deadly allergic to all three; carrots, raisins, and nuts. After they wiped the blood off his shocked face, I tried to offer him some cake, but sadly, he declined.

The police arrived when I finished the third slice of cake; I remember wanting a glass of milk, but there was blood on my hands, and I didn't want to get the fridge dirty.

Maybe I should have asked an adult, but they seemed somewhat indisposed at the time.

I don't remember much after going upstairs to shower and head to bed. I could hear screaming as I pulled the covers over my head, but I think that's normal after watching something traumatic.

It took them a few days to realize that I was still in the house, and a bit longer to find someone to take me in.

My grandparents were the ones to take me in.

My grandmother was also a drinker. But she turned to gardening rather than violence.

She was different; she walked around the house with the random bruises given to her by my grandfather and his siblings. She was quiet, hardly saying a word while they beat her.

I don't know if she was strong or too far gone to care anymore. I gave her a gun for her 81st birthday.

A year after I had left the house to travel, I heard she had killed all of them. I felt a bit proud of her.

Just like my mom, if she pushed hard enough, she could also do it. Taking life with a smile.

A Pirate by Another Name

A Short Story by Jona Nightingale

A low groan came from the floorboards, then a hacking of lungs. But that, too, was normal at the Vagabond Bar.

Drunks would often fall to the ground when the beer was too good or the times too rough to handle. The Vagabond Bar was a place where the dregs of society would gather and tell a tale or two.

If you stayed long enough, you would hear of the pirates who claimed the sea as their home. The brutal souls who would kill at the drop of a hat. The pirates whose flags still haunted the navy with their cruelty and wanton nature.

The tales would start with an argument, of course, about who had been the worst of their kind. Some would yell Black Beard and others, Davey Jones, but a few remembered a pirate so cruel, that the navy made their name illegal to say. Even the navy had joined hands with the crown to jail any soul who dared to utter the name of Ira, The Devourer.

She had been a fearsome opponent, with a ship that could rival all the pirates combined. Some say with her mind alone she commanded the vessel on which she sailed.

Others whispered that her ship was haunted and so was she.

But everything they knew about the Ira, The Devourer was pure speculation. It had been 10 years since they saw her crimson flag flowing in the wind.

Rumor has it, that a storm that not even the best pirates could not have survived captured her vessel and took it down to the sea floor for a proper burial. The navy had stated that she had been captured and would stand trial for her crimes on the high sea against the crown.

By the time the date of the trial arrived, the Navy had still yet to present Ira to the public. They were made a laughingstock for their arrogance and audacity. Instead of Ira facing the gallows, two commanding officers responsible for her arrest hung like dried fruit in the wind.

The pirates rejoiced, their hero had yet to die, but she did not return to the sea. And so rumors began to surface.

Ira, The Devourer was taken by the sea.

Ira, The Devourer was held captive by the crown.

Ira, The Devourer haunted the shipyard at night looking for lazy sailors.

Ira.

Ira.

Ira.

Ira lay in a puddle of her own vomit, not particularly her best night at the bar, but it was still far from her worst.

At her best, Ira was taller than most, with broad shoulders and dark skin that glowed in the sun but rendered her invisible at night if she wanted to be. Her hair hung free from her shoulders wrapped in scarves and carried little trinkets attached to the ends. She always kept her treasure close in a pouch she wore around her waist.

Ira wore vibrant colors and could make the sea roll with her laughter, but the best thing about her was her ability to find the silver lining in even the worst situations. As she picked herself off the floor and looked about the bar, she was having a hard time finding a silver lining in this particular situation.

So Ira drank until drinking was all she knew, not the sea, or treasure. Just a bottle to her lips.

She knew that drinking her problems away was an inefficient way to resolve them, but at least it tasted good, and the hangovers were less now. Though being dead could be a reason for that, she didn't feel like dwelling on the small details today.

It could also be that even if she could find her way to the bar, they were separated by two different realms. She could see the pirates and miscreants of society drinking the night away, but she could not actually drink with them.

She was a prisoner in a cage made by her own greed and idiocy.

Ira had always wanted to be a pirate, one that was revered throughout history. But dreams were so hard to come by these days, with so many people wanting them and giving so little effort back to the dreams we never really think about.

Ira should have asked questions, but who really asks questions when a little lady stands before you with a smile and says she will grant your dream on condition?

"Yes," Ira said a bit too loud in the middle of the night, "Let my dreams happen."

She should have stopped herself at that point, and remembered what they told her about sea witches tempting would-be sailors into bargains they could not afford to lose.

But Ira did not stop, she stood there with a huge grin on her face as if she was on top of the world. And at that moment she was, her dreams were about to come true.

The terms of the contract were only revealed to Ira after their lips collided in a passionate kiss. She yanked her head away from the woman as the taste of blood filled her mouth. When, Ira could not hold it in anymore and spat it out on the walkway.

Red splashes of blood glared back at her as she stared in disbelief at the woman who had just stolen her first kiss.

"What's this? WHAT DID YOU DO?" Bellowed Ira as she tried to wipe the remnants of the kiss and blood away.

"What did I do? I granted your wish. I only took my compensation early." Cooed the woman who began to look more like a creature from the depths of the ocean with her gills and turquoise skin.

Blood pooled in Ira's mouth and dripped from her ears as she tried to wipe it away with her sleeves.

"Make it stop," she begged as the pain became worse and blood leaked from her nose and ears.

The old lady cackled as she revealed her true form.

A sea witch.

The witch unfurled herself from the form she had taken, growing into a mountain of bones and ships discarded by the ocean. Her eyes were crimson red and her fingers turned to long claws that scraped along the pathway.

Ira looked on in horror as the taste of iron filled her mouth and blood trickled down the corners of her lips.

She knew it then, she was dying.

Her life flashed before her eyes; the funeral of her parents, how her aunts discarded her, the smell of the ocean, taking her first drink with her captain.

She remembered it all.

A scream so fearsome and vile, something pulled itself from the depths of her soul as she tried to break the contract.

The wind whipped at her hair and the clouds rolled across the sky as lightening struck the ground in front of her. Ira summoned all the strength left in her body, but it wasn't enough.

No amount of inner strength could save her from the mistake she had made. She was dying and there was nothing she could do about it.

Ira glared at the witch that was as tall as a mouth, "So what will you give me for taking my life." Venom soaked her voice, for she could no longer hide her fury.

In a split moment, she had ceased being frustrated at herself and now turned all her rage towards the witch.

"Power. Your ship will never run out of cannons, your sails will always find the wind, your crew will never desert you. On the seven seas, your name will be known and feared."

While Ira could not fully see the face of the witch, she was sure a smug hung on her lips. She boasted of power and notoriety, what Ira had always wanted but held back in fear of what she would lose.

Her father would say, *The price of power is as steep as a cliff by the sea.*

She finally understood what he meant. Her vision began to blur as she grew dizzy. Ira tried her best to remain awake, to fight one last time against the heavy feeling that slipped through her bones and rendered her useless.

She had been too late, "A fool, to trust Itha's words. Blessings and curses, come with a burden."

She murmured these words as her last resort.

"A burden I give back to the giver, a blessing, and curse."

The mountain cracked at her words, trembling before small chunks of rock began to fall away. Bit by bit, they fell into the air and became a part of the wind that whipped through the docks and alleyways.

Ira was already dead when the witch crumbled away, screaming curses at Ira for the burden she had been given.

Despite Ira only knowing of the sea, she knew the one thing that could damage a sea witch.

A gift for a gift, a curse for a curse, a blessing for a blessing.

The balance of the seas must always remain. It was the oath of a sea witch.

As the years went by, Ira's dreams came true. She was a fearsome pirate, disregarding all laws and rules. There was a saying, "Nothing stays untouched in the path of Ira, The Devourer."

Ira became the ruler of the seas with a cruel grip. She did not take prisoners, all who came into her path were blown to pieces and left for dead. She did not seek treasure, she left it all at sea. What she truly sought was how to undo the curse that took her life.

She searched far and wide for the sea witch that had granted her wish and thus made her an immortal ghost that haunted the seas rather than enjoyed the feel of the ocean that surrounded her.

Of course, it had its perks, you never went hungry, your ship was always in perfect condition. But it lacked any challenge.

There were no rivals on the sea, just lesser pirates that wanted revenge. They would sometimes try to group together and try to ambush Ira, but the wind told her their secrets.

It whispered to her on the calmest of nights and through the roughest weather. Ever since that night, the wind became her friend, her confidant, her comrade on the high seas. But it wasn't just the wind. Ira carried the hopes of all sailors and pirates alike that loved the sea.

She was one of the few souls that could still interact with the living and tell the tale. The years when Ira ruled the seas had been kind to her, her crew loved the adventures that came their way, the monsters that they fought, the treasures they found, the navy they continued to evade.

But dreams sometimes die when you least expect them to.

Like wind drifting from her sails, Ira found out her dreams had changed, she wanted to live on land in a small cottage by the ocean. Perhaps she had grown tired of the monotonous routine her life had followed.

It did not matter.

Because as soon as her dream changed, the curse broke. The blessing was gone, and the gift was no longer.

A veil appeared in front of her, she could no longer interact with the living.

At first, it didn't matter. The navy told the world they had captured her and boasted of her execution. But how do you capture a ghost? So Ira watched as they scrambled to prove their words and chuckled to herself when the two commanders hung by their necks like dried fruit in the wind.

It didn't matter when she could no longer taste the rum in her favorite bar, or when they told ghost stories of how she haunted the seas with her crew.

It didn't matter that she was slowly becoming even more famous than when she sailed the seas and rained terror in the hearts of sailors and pirates alike.

It didn't matter.

It didn't matter.

It didn't matter.

Until it was too late.

Until Ira realized that her dream had outgrown her, and she could never tell her story. She was no a fable, a myth, a legend, a story to tell the children as they went to bed at night.

Ira had lived and died a pirate, but now that she was dead, she could not enjoy the silence and peace of death.

It might have been because she never found the witch that granted her wish, or how she drifted listlessly through the alleyways and ignore the rowdy bars filled with life and excitement.

Sam, a friendly ghost, had found her wandering the streets late at night as he left his local haunting spot. He had been a ghost for more than a century, and he had learned a few things about how to live as a proper ghost.

It was in the minor details, most ghost lost their purpose upon dying and wandered around until given a new goal in death.

Truthfully, it wasn't their fault. Few people were prepared for existing after death. To most, it was a shock to still exist in any realm.

Sam didn't blame them. He pitied them for their lack of preparation. That's why he had taken it upon himself to help the wandering ghosts and give them a purpose. Something more than haunting, but less than letting the wind drag them around.

Most ghosts never realize that the wind was not their friend. The wind was only kind to sailors and pirates alike. And only when they were on the open sea.

Once a pirate or sailor returned to land, the wind was like a curse. Never a gift or a blessing.

Sam had known a thing or two about Ira before he met her that night. He had known that she was one of the most fearsome pirates in history only followed by the worst of the dead. Rumor had it that Black Beard was her second in command. But no one could prove it seeing as the living was never allowed on her ship.

A ship for the dead by the dead.

It was the dream of many and Ira had granted it with her wish. But when she lost the desire to keep her dream alive, it was more than her who lost their way.

Now was the perfect moment for Sam to shine, or perhaps dull the blow of death just a bit more for the misplaced pirates.

Since he had a lot of free time, he had started an organization of sorts.

"The Grim: Finding meaning in the afterlife."

By the dead, for the dead.

The principle was simple. Sam took in the newly dead and trained them to exist beyond death. His team grew with each passing year, some might even say he created a monopoly on the afterlife.

He gave the dead a reason to make their existence a joyful one. Some went on to haunt their loved ones or the people that hurt them. Others were worshiped as gods, and there were those who expanded the foundation of Grim.

Soon after Sam began to spread his philosophy, Grim agencies were found all over the world with no true leader but a collective goal—to make the afterlife a meaningful existence.

Sam found his passion in scaring the locals that went to the Logan Bar. He would place orders that had yet to be carried to their table and occasionally trip a passerby. But the locals loved it, it gave them something to look forward to in the evenings.

The docks that once bustled with life had only rustled with the embers of excitement now. This was a ghost town on the best of days and a misery of an existence on the worst days.

Perhaps that's why Ira liked to lose herself in this town. They only whispered of her existence here. She was a figment of their imagination, a mystery, a legend.

Some days, she began to question if she was ever real. Did she ever truly live her life before it was taken away from her?

At this point, she couldn't remember what life meant for her in the years before her dream became a curse.

She doesn't remember, but Ira was happy. So full of life and determined to be the best pirate that ever ruled the sea. Sure, she would get into the occasional scuffle, but nothing that was worth involving the guards to resolve. She was strong for her age, a mere 17 years she had lived before the curse changed her.

These thoughts lingered on her mind as she wandered the alleyways in the wee hours of the morning. She thought of death and what it meant to lose yourself in the dream you've always wanted.

Ira wanted to feel the urge to dream again. She had to, her entire crew had lost their purpose in roaming the sea. She had been their purpose, their only goal and idol.

Ira wanted to cry, but the tears felt less like tears and more like the wind whispering. She could not bear to feel the wind lap at her face. She had no right to crave anything that reminded her of the sea.

In her misery, Ira bumped into Sam. It's more accurate to say that her existence nudged against his. A very unpleasant feeling ran through her as a shiver climbed along her back.

The dead were like that, avoiding the discomfort of touch with their entire being. They would recoil at the touch of another ghost or existence. Sure, they could touch things, but never each other without feeling disgusted.

Some dead liked that feeling, their justification was that touch required some sacrifice to let them connect with each other. While others used it as a means to torture a soul as it wandered without guidance.

Ira had learned early on to only touch another soul when it was absolutely required, and nothing more than that. You could lose yourself in the desire for connection and end up in one of the places the Grim society never tells you about.

The dead weren't the only ones of this side of the veil, and occasionally they would forget that.

Ira learned the truth about the veil from her mother when she was younger. Her mother was what you might call a cursed child. Her fate was tangled delicately with the unfortunate occurrences of the world. She would wander into a disaster just as it was about to unfold. The cart she rode on would bring a plague.

A drought would begin as soon as she stepped into a region. It just happened that way. And yet, she had a way of bringing blessings to the places she left. Ira's mother was a stocky woman with dark brown hair and eyes like a sparrow. She was built sturdy, as if life knew what struggles she would have to hold on her shoulders.

Through her travels, she taught Ira the importance of paying attention to the little things. If a leaf moved too quickly in the wind, it was being carried. You could only have one shadow, but if you happen to have three or four, be kind to them for the day.

Ira remembered all of these sayings as if her mother were whispering them to her as she looked at Sam. It was not death flashing before her eyes, but the splendor of life intertwining with her fate.

Sam stood under the light of a lantern, and you could tell how tall he had truly been when he was alive. The color of his hair was washed out now, but it had been black like the night and the same skin tone had shimmered like silver in the light.

Ira looked at him closer, observing the crook of his nose or how his eyes never truly looked into to hers but, he seemed to understand that she was lost. Perhaps more lost than she had let herself believe. But Sam had a knack for doing that, seeing the soul.

"You should come with me." He said it like a command and not a suggestion.

Usually Sam was calm, even aloof, but he looked away with an intensity in his eyes that had haunted his younger days. He was not used to feeling the pull of another on his soul like that.

Of course, it had happened to him before, four times at least, but it happened so rarely that he nearly forgot the feeling until it lingered on his mind like a distant memory.

Now, with the feeling of his soul crying out so loudly, he would have cried if he could. But the dead lost their ability to cry half a century after being dead. There was an exception of course, if you chose to become a wailing ghost, something between a witch and a banshee. You kept your ability to cry, but you would have lost something else.

Even in death, the balance must remain equal.

Ira followed after Sam, finding herself pulled in his direction by some great force. She had hoped she followed him out of a compulsion to find another ghost to speak with, and not the nudging in her mind that told her the answer she sought was with him.

Sam led her through the winding alleyways and down into the catacombs of the town. Far beneath the earth where the past was forgotten laid a box with her true name on it.

A ghost true name mean many things, but it had more to do with finding the essence of their soul than with their dreams and wishes.

They did not need to a light as their eyes naturally adjusted to the dark. Spiders crawled along the walls as mice scurried past them. The air, if they could smell it, was stuffy with the stench of decay. They glided to a closed room and passed through the wall.

"That box is for you, from your mother." Sam spoke in a monotone voice, as if all the emotion had been discarded from his being.

Ira did not understand. But it was one of the few things she remembered about her mother, other than her being cursed by misfortune. Her mother always carried a wooden box with her. It was made from the tree in her hometown, but the hinges were golden, and the lock was a metal only royalty would use.

It was one of the many distinctions of the social classes.

Pirates, the dregs of humanity, did not mix with royalty, except it was a pirate hanging with a rope around their neck.

But there was even one more exception to the rule.

If you just so happen to be a cursed royal, expelled from the castle due to your ability to cause misfortune wherever you went. And you just so happen to find a pirate that loves the excitement of your misfortunes.

A pirate and royal, well ex-royal, can indeed fall in love and have a child while giving up the sea to wander from town to town.

It would also explain the name Ira.

Ira.

But what if that ex-royal also had the blood of a witch running through her veins. Not just any witch, but a sea witch as tall as a mountain with a knack for making unfair deals.

If said royal, had then taught her daughter about what happens behind the veil and what it means to live with the unknown.

Ira.

And if that pirate planted a dream within you to sail the seas and rule over it as a king. As he once did.

Then perhaps you would find yourself drunk on pride and ego, guided by greed to demand of such a sea witch. Not for the life of your parents, who were taken by a plague, leaving you without a family and a home. You would ask for your father's wish and using your mother's tongue to make it all come true.

Ira.

Despite all the obvious clues that were left behind by her parents, Ira had just realized the gravity of the box that sat so delicately on the dingy table in front of her.

Perhaps Sam was a part of the trail of crumbs that would lead her here. Ira began to wonder if her mother had known that she was a foolish child and would die before she had made her name in the world.

She stepped forward, holding her breath, if a ghost had such a thing, and wiped of the dust that had settled on the lid of the box.

Irene Niedel Von Randeil

That was Ira's true name.

She knew it as soon as she saw it. It was custom to give a child a nickname until they were old enough to know of the strength and power of a true name.

Only your parents and spouse could know your true name. They could not tell another even if they wanted to; they were bound by the rules of this realm.

But the ghost realm was different. You could know the true name of another. It was still deemed taboo, but a few ghosts liked to deal with the taboo and dark arts.

Ghosts would sometimes sit together like the gossiping aunts in a village, telling each other the true names they had found out recently. They were troublesome things, but at least they had found their purpose in the afterlife, so most souls left them alone with their gossip.

However, Ira had never really cared for the true name of another, she had other thoughts to keep her company like plundering and robbing the navy.

Ira did not leave the tomb after she had received her true name, rather she stayed there for more than two months as she recalled the memories of her past. She wanted to put together what little she knew of her parents into a moment in time that she could understand.

Many nights she found herself lingering near the bones of a ghost long gone. While she might have wanted to give her parent's story back to the light of day, she didn't really know if what she felt was right.

Ira had been so disconnected from her emotions for so long that she could not tell that she was feeling regret. It was perhaps the most human thing Ira had done in years since her death. But seeing as it was a foreign emotion to her, it made Ira feel uncomfortable.

She began to recount her faults and failures in the last few years.

That was the thing with regret and emotions after death, you can either move on from them, or you can wallow in it. Ira had decided to wallow. She had nothing but time on her hands, an eternity to figure out her true dream once more.

The thought of finding out her true dream was what moved Ira from the tomb and back into the realm of ghosts with a purpose. Sure, Ira had yet to find her dream once more, but now she was curious about what it meant to have a dream in the first place.

With a bit of effort and skill, she was able to retrace her steps to the place Sam called home.

For the first time since meeting Sam, Ira asked him a question.

"What did it mean to dream?"

Sam face scrunched up like a piece of paper as he thought about what she might be actually asking.

"Are you talking about when you sleep at night or when you find something to desire?"

Ira sat down on the floor of Sam's sitting room and thought about this for a moment. She had not noticed how the house was furnished with gold and ivory trimmings, or how it seemed so sophisticated for a ghost dwelling. Sam's place was well taken cared of without him having to do much about it. Ira let her mind wander for a while as she thought about what it meant to dream.

She knew then that she was talking about desire. As she lost her will to live the life she had been granted, Ira lost her will to desire something only for herself.

In this instance, Ira was torn. She wanted to live out the rest of her years finding out the story of her parents and what truly happened to them; yet the sea called to her like an old lover. Even the wind, known for its distaste of those who dwelled on land, whispered to her to return to the sea.

Ira still had an entire crew that waited upon her return to the sea. She knew that as soon as she drifted off the land, her ship would appear under her and her crew would be dragged back to the ship.

It had always been that way, Ira was destined to roam the seas and she knew it. Her ship was more of an idea, she simply willed it into existence. And as she placed the pieces together in her mind, her crew came along with it. Her wish was their command.

Yet, her mind still faltered in the years since she had been lost.

A kite without direction or the wind to give her the lift she needed.

So here she sat, in Sam's sitting room, realizing just how far she had drifted off course.

"Desire."

Sam saw the revelation that slowly began to build in her words. He had a way of noticing such things, when souls began to move forward after being trapped for so long.

"To desire is to want something. Perhaps you desire something you once had or a new dream that reminds you of the past." Sam's words were kind, as if he were talking to a friend.

Sam watched Ira's face light up like a vacant house that had been deserted. He saw the candlelight flicker in the windows of her soul and the hearth blaze once more. The fireplace had kindling and then the clashing of stones in the quiet of the night. Her soul had embers of hope and purpose.

A small smile lingered on Sam's lips. He had saved another lost soul. Maybe not fully, but the process had truly begun.

"What do you desire?"

"The sea."

"How?"

"To sail it and discover its beauty and treasures."

"Why?"

"Because it is my inheritance."

Ira knew it then, she had spoken the truth.

She was the daughter of a pirate and the granddaughter of a sea witch. Where could she call home if not the sea? Sure, her life on the land had been interesting, but it often paled in comparison to the waves that crashed against her ship late at night.

They simply could not compare, sure it had its mysteries and hidden beauty. But the sea had her heart.

"Does this mean I must now return to the sea?"

"Right now?" Sam asked. He was a bit amused at how she seemed to be lost and found at the same time.

"You don't have to go back there right now. Why don't you take the time to figure out more of your desire?"

Ira took his question into consideration, sure she had time, plenty of it, actually. But she didn't know exactly where to start.

She no longer wanted the name of Ira, The Devourer to follow her as she claimed the sea as her home. It has been too daunting. She would find it a hard time to explore the remnants of her heritage with that name.

As Ira began to mull over Sam's words in her head, she forgot one very important fact. Her ship and the horror it conveyed was an idea. All she had to do was change what she wanted her ship to look like and it would comply.

The only caveat was her crew remained the same, but they could be taught how to act in the coming years. Ira could be a merchant ship, bringing goods to those who needed it. Yet she had never been really kind to the merchants before.

But she could start right this moment.

Something like Spousal Abuse

A Short Story by Jona Nightingale

The first time my wife hit me, it was on our 7th anniversary in August. She had been in a low mood and I, ever the clown, had made it my business to cheer her up.

She did not find me amusing that night.

I was on the floor, passed out before I had finished telling my third joke. There are blood stains where the ashtray connected to my face and broke my nose, granting me five stitches.

"It was an accident," she cried as the paramedics wheeled me away. And it was at first. But by the eighth time, I knew she wanted to do nothing more than hurt me.

Her rage became a weapon, the thing that strangled me in my dreams, I would lay awake gasping for air and her words would find me in the dark. Sweet caring words, but I knew the truth.

In the dark, she could pretend that her rage would not take her again. Pretend it did not contort her face to something unrecognizable.

September came and went, and all the months followed with the ambulance and emergency room knowing me by name.

I would tell them that it was an accident, but I knew the truth. The stitches told me a different story, when she stopped apologizing, her eyes still met mine with a look of regret and disgust.

I could not tell if it was then the worst of everything began.

Did she hate me?

Do I think of her as a monster as well?

I stared at her long enough to know the difference between an accident and general intent. She smiled then, a sweet, seductive smile.

One that would normally make my heart race thinking of how I was so lucky.

Now my heart raced for a different reason.

I knew that she meant every hit, every word that pierced my smile and my armor. The subtle sense of dread crept into our home and stayed.

Most people would have left then, I was not like most people. I wanted to believe that she could change, back to something less violent and monster-like.

I stopped hoping when she broke my right leg. I started praying for strength as it healed.

That's the funny thing about life, you never know when love will change to something darker. Something meaner.

My wife looked at me and smiled, as if to nod her approval for the depth of my sorrow. She smiled as I grieved our relationship.

Her smile haunted me, and told me I was nothing. Far too small to find my way back to the people we once were.

The rage in me started from a small wink as she stuck a needle in my arm.

Why was I the abused?

Why had I stayed?

Was I not stronger than her?

Why did she not love me?

Each moment brought more questions, why was I not good enough for the gentle affection she promised me in the beginning?

Was it all a lie?

I didn't leave.

I stayed.

For six more months, I took every hit and stitch that went along my jaw and legs. I stayed because I wanted to even the scales once more.

I waited for our anniversary once more, and acted like I was less than human. Took every comment and hit with the grace of a merchant entertaining the imperial court.

I made her dinner that night. Her favorite. Smoked lamb ravioli with a creamy mushroom sauce.

The dining room was lit with beautiful, calming candles, and I watched her choke on the poison I fed her.

Shock, then resignation, tumbled across her face like rag weeds. She knew what was coming.

When she woke up strapped to a chair and her feet soaked in water, she smiled at me. Not her seductive smile, but the one that never reached her eyes. The one I was used to.

I waited for her face to contort, for her to start yelling. The fear sat heavily in my body from months of conditioning.

When nothing happened, she started to laugh. Loud and booming laughter filled the basement. I did not back away, but I was tempted to shrink and make myself smaller.

I was tempted to run upstairs and out the door into the heat of summer and never return.

My bags were already packed, my ticket booked, and all I needed was to leave.

And yet I stayed, I wanted to finish what I started for the very last time.

"You think this," my wife spoke to me for the first time in weeks as she scanned the room. "Will free you of me?"

"You idiot, you actually think you will ever be free of me?" Her words landed like slaps across my face. "You will live the rest of your life eaten by regret. I will ahh-"

Her screams filled the room as a hammer slammed down on her fingers. This time, I had no intention of backing away. Her words had already broken me, and it was not my responsibility to show her what brokenness looked like.

I had given her all my faith and trust, but now, I was nothing more than a mangled mannequin.

"YOU PSYCHOTIC BI-AHH—"

I would not let her get another word in. The hammer came down over and over again. Her fingers were mangled pieces of bone, a sinew.

The next hand got the same treatment as her feet. When she passed out from the pain, I opened her mouth with pliers and a metal gag, so I could pull her teeth out one by one.

I gave her painkillers and woke her up, she gargled her words. Drool ran down her face and the fear that had sat in the corner of my soul, dragged its dark whispers through her mind.

She was no longer angry as she began to dry heave all the poison I had fed her in the last few months.

It was already too late.

Nothing was going to stop me from removing her from this world.

I pulled her teeth that night, one by one, until all 30 of them lay on the floor.

Rivers of blood ran down the chair as she fainted from the pain once more. She was dying, I knew that. My goal was her death, and here I felt remorse clawing at the back of my throat.

Her breath was shallow, ragged even, and I waited for the last hope to leave her lungs. I could have turned back at that moment, stopped what I was doing, and saved her.

The hero who found my wife after coming home late from work. I had all my alibis ready and waiting.

I could not do it, could not stop myself from puncturing her heart and watching the blood ooze out.

A hollow feeling filled my chest, as I let my wife die by my hands. Her body was still warm as I took it from the house and strapped her into the car.

I wanted nothing more than to care for her then, to wipe her tears and make her laugh.

Just to tell her one more joke, as the joy slipped from her face and the hate replaced the smile lines.

To watch the rage she had been trained to show and the bruises she had been instructed to give.

And now, I will never hear that bemoaned voice of resignation as I told her my plan for us to die together.

The drive into the ocean was nicer than we had thought in the end. It was calm.

Mama's Boy

A Short Story by Jona Nightingale

The damp air clung to my skin on the late Georgian summer night, and I sighed with the respite of a factory worker getting off their double shift.

Crickets made music; some made love as the man before me tried to crawl away. He was doing a terrible job at it.

His left leg was broken in two places; I had made sure of it, as he had once used that same leg to step on my mother's back as he mugged her.

I was not generally drawn to vengeance, but to the little old lady who raised me when I was just a rag-tag of problems. I would do anything to see that she was taken care of.

The man groaned as I walked forward. Rolling my shoulders, I no longer took in the night air or felt comfortable in my own skin.

I knew my actions were against the law, but that didn't matter. I took the needle from my shirt pocket and filled it with a small concoction of mercury, melatonin, and a saline solution.

My lovely mother had asked me to give her attacker a slow and agonizing death, and I had always been an obedient son.

Carefully, I held him still as he struggled against me and injected him. Then, with much more delicacy than I thought capable, I wrapped his mangled, whizzing body into a large tarp and rolled him into a ditch.

Someone was bound to find him in a few days, but by then, he would have starved to death with the terrible memory of all his misdeeds known.

I drove away from that summer night with a smile on my face and proud to be a mama's boy.

And a damn obedient one at that.

A Fool's Errand

A Short Story by Jona Nightingale

Susan crawled to the phone; her legs, she could tell, were broken in at least three places. The fall was sudden, but in her old age, she had become more of a klutz.

The box had not been there when she first walked through the hall, and as she stomped about. It was ready and waiting.

Tears rolled down her face, but the phone was close enough that she just had a bit more to go. It wasn't one of those smartphones; she had never learned how to use one, and she had been too stubborn to learn how.

Perhaps that's why she did not see the figure walk up behind her. Nor did she hear the fall of the heavy footsteps as they moved the box out of the way to where it was before they had made their little plan.

Susan's hand reached for the phone and pulled down on the table to sit a little closer. All she had to do was call for an ambulance and stay awake for them. The pain felt all-consuming as it radiated up and down her legs. Maybe it was broken in more than three places; she couldn't tell.

The figure moved to a darkened corner and watched her call for help. It watched as she struggled for words, and it smiled when she cried out in pain.

It was a small smile, and then it was on the edge of gleeful laughter. The figure had to cover its mouth, unwilling to give itself away and ruin the game it had started.

Poor Susan hung on to the words of the operator like a lifeline. Her adrenaline started to fade as her mind told her she had finished all she had set out to do. The feeling of sleep washed over her and threatened to take her under.

The operator began to call her name, "Susan? Susan? Are you still there? An ambulance is on the way." They tried to offer her reassurance and a bit of hope.

After all, an operator's job was to provide guidance and support until someone else could get there.

The figure shifted in the shadows and stepped forward to hang up the phone.

"Sorry for the call; I'll take care of her now." It did not wait for the operator to oppose or ask who else was there.

Susan hung on the edge of sleep but smiled up at the figure.

"I almost got away this time." She said, with a lull. And she had almost escaped from its clutches, but the figure had been craftier than she could ever imagine.

Sirens blared in the background as the figure looked down at her and winked.

Susan smiled, "I hope you can convince them this time, too." Her eyes sparkled with mischief before sleep overtook her.

The figure bent down and picked up her body before throwing her over its shoulder and returning to her room.

Her room had all the decorations she had when she was fifteen. The Rolling Stones posters lined the wall, with knick-knacks of the 60s she had long forgotten.

The figure laid her down, gave her a sedative and a shot of probiotics, and tucked her in. Later, it would have to fix her legs, but for now, emergency personnel were pounding on the door.

It smiled once more as the caretaker of the Mary Hester Shelter opened the door.

Saheem and The Little Black Book

A Short Story by Jona Nightingale

Saheem's hands worn from mistreatment and fear shook in the darkness, gripping the small book tighter.

The desert wind rolled across the dunes, blowing cold air into the night. There were no lights here, no wandering traveler, no village that he could rest his head for the night. Just him, the clothes on his back, and a little black book.

He pulled his hoodie closer to his body and walked on, dragging his feet throw the sand in hope of warmth. By the time he saw a light peaking out of the sand dunes, he had cried three times and his phone had long died.

Forgetting his dreary body, Saheem screamed and ran as fast as he could towards the light. Slowly buildings began to form in the distance, a small village was tucked in the valley of the desert.

Red and blue roofs laid checkered throughout the village as noise rose from the vibrant night market.

Saheem felt his mouth begin to water the closer he drew to the village. Scents of sweet and salty dishes and bread lingered in the night air.

He pictured warm plates of food and a hot bath. He longed for a soft bed to rest his head and lay his aching bones to ease. The village was situated in the corner of what looked like a mountain, but that had to be impossible.

It was impossible for there to be a mountain in the middle of a desert. Saheem scurried across the dunes like a rat looking for their next meal. His tattered clothes and scarf hung on his frame like old rags left to their own devices.

Before he could reach the village his voice gave out, then his legs, swiftly followed by his conscience. His body laid in the sand slowly sinking as the night rolled on, wiping away all traces of his struggle to find a warm bath and a place to be at ease.

Saheem woke to the sound of laughter. His head pounded with a fierceness that rivaled the gods.

Covering his eyes to shield them from the light, he struggled to sit up straight. Sharp pains shot through his rib cage, sending him clattering back to the mat. The laughter stopped, turning into worried tones as a woman's voice called out to him.

"Miss, don't move around so much, you'll shift your bandages!" Her voice grew closer, and a woman wearing light cloth tossed about her body appeared, grabbing his sides and assessing his wounds as she tossed him back and forth.

"The healer said if you had been a weaker woman, you would have surely died." Saheem hissed at her words and turned his gaze away from hers.

"I am no woman," he mumbled under his breath as he reached for the bindings on his chest. They weren't there, his hand brushed against the soft tissue of his chest and he gasped, looking down at his body for the first time since he had regained consciousness.

Except for the bandages that covered his wounds, Saheem had laid in the presence of women naked as the day he was born. He tried to stand to his feet hastily once more, only to be dragged back down to the ground by what seem to be women.

Saheem scanned the room, taking in the bathhouse, women of all sizes crowded around him whispering in low hushed tones. Frantically, he tried once more to escape their gazes, but his plan was foiled by the women that had held him down.

The onlookers snickered at his attempt, "You would do a better job resting than trying to escape. You are lucky we found you before the scavengers could."

Saheem closed his eyes tightly, refusing to look at the woman that had spoken or any of the women in the bathhouse for that matter. It would be quite indecent for him to peek at them since they had mistaken him for a woman despite his bound chest and obvious beard.

"Where are my things? What happened to my clothes and the book I carried?" His anger began to boil over as rifts of frustration bleed into his voice. Saheem clutched his fist and screamed out for the seventh time today, "Little book, free me from this wretched curse already!"

The women looked around at each other before they began to whisper amongst themselves once more.

Stranger

Monster

The defiled

Saheem screamed once more, "Little book, honor your promise and take me back." He continued to scream the same sentence until his voice became coarse, and the women drew back in fear. Their whispers became louder, slurs flew about like water.

Yet Saheem refused to shed a tear, he had become used to these words even in his home, how could a stranger hurt him now.

He began to tremble once more, but this time it was neither from the chill of the desert nor the fear of never returning home. The tremor was from the anger that grew with each murmur that he caught.

Inhaling sharply, he lunged forward, this time slipping through the grasps of the women that held him still.

Saheem dove headfirst into the bath, pushing past the bystanders that stood and pointed with twisted faces. He dove deep into the water, screaming curses in his mind at the little book.

Just as the water current began to shift his weight, a force yanked him through the water, knocking him unconscious once more.

He awoke, clutching a little black book to his chest and breathing heavily. Saheem had returned to his room in the attic. If he had not experienced this feeling before, he would have passed it off as a dream.

Yet, if he dared to open the little black book he would have found an old wrinkled check and the word desert scratched out with red ink, just like the previous words before it.

It had become his curse; to live in a place that would never accept him and a check he could not spend.

And a little black book that was hell-bent on sending him to the depths of the universe hunting for a treasure he could never dream of.

My ragged words

A Short Story by Jona Nightingale

"You look like a whale." He said.

I did not look at him then or when he brought the knife to my throat and poked it against the flesh. Tiny drops of blood rolled down my neck.

I wanted to scream.

To tell him what I thought of him and his authority, to watch him beg for salvation as I took the knife away and bleed him dry.

I did nothing but shiver at the idea that he would never leave me alone long enough for me to grow in my anger. I sat in my seat and looked at the floor, daydreaming about a braver version of myself, a version that he could not hurt.

"Did you hear what I said, whale?" He asked, voice shaking with rage.

I knew I should have answered him then, but the rage swelled in me like a tide, and I wanted nothing more than to let this tsunami of silence wash him away.

He moves closer, grabbing my neck and pulling the blade away. "You better answer when I talk to you!" His hot breath, riddled by years of decay, blasts against my face, and I try to pull away.

"You worthless piece of shit, you think I won't hit you." His voice is a jolly combination of rage and satisfaction. "You think I won't break all the bones in your body and watch you bleed out."

My voice catches in my throat, and I reach up with a wayward determination to claw at his hands.

I don't want this, I whisper in my mind. I don't want this pain or the fear in my chest anymore.

Before I can reach up to take his hand away. Pain radiates from my cheek and I can feel my skin bruising as he hits me over and over again. I want to hide, to shield my face, but the hits come hard and fast.

"You useless bitch! You think you're better than me, don't you?"

My ears are ringing, and I try to make myself small, to protect the little piece of dignity that I have left.

It doesn't work.

I cry out in pain; words fall from my lips, begging him to stop hitting me, show mercy on my soul, and love me instead of hating me.

That's when I see it. The knife, just waiting for me. It called my name like an old friend. I had enough scars to know the sharpness of the blade intimately.

I reached out with all my courage and grabbed the blade. He did not see me in his fit of rage. He overlooked my lunge towards his ankle and thought I would cling to him again.

The blade lodged into his skin and ripped through the flesh. His screams turned to cursing as he fumbled to the floor.

I dragged myself away from him, hiding the knife. I smeared his blood over my mouth and pretended that I had bitten him.

His gaze was horrified and then filled with rage. The world stood still around me as I held my breath and waited; my heart did not try to break the chains that held it in my chest.

He charged towards me, "YOU FUCKING BITCH!"

The air fled from my lungs, and I steadied myself against the chair. I waited until he was close enough until my heart and mind were calm.

Then, as if all the world slowed down and waited for me, I pulled the blade from behind my back, dug it into his throat, and twisted.

He looked at me in horror as he realized what I had done. His hands flew to his neck to try to stop the bleeding.

But it was too late, I knew I had done a good job. I looked at him as he thrashed about, trying to scream, but only blood rattled around in his lungs.

He was dying, slow and agonizing, as he had promised my death would be.

I watched him fade, with a glimmer of hope in my eyes and a smile on my lips. And with the last of my strength, I spoke for the first time since the abuse started, "I am not worthless."

My voice was ragged with the bruises from a decade of torture, but it worked.

The day I left

A Short Story by Jona Nightingale

Blood pooled on the floor, and I tried to look away from my father as he lay there begging.

I did not want to watch him die, but I did.

I watched his pleading eyes as his blood soaked through the carpet and stained the wood underneath.

My mother would not be happy, though I doubt she would be unhappy to see her husband die.

Their marriage was not my problem. My leaving was.

I walked around the blood, making sure not to get any on my shoes.

My bags were at the door, waiting for me to leave this place.

Then I heard the stairs squeak with the confirmed certainty of someone watching. My eyes landed on my mother's blood-soaked form, and I knew what happened.

The entire scene had first confused me; how had my father found his way onto a knife seven times? As much as I wished I was the one who did it, the deed was beyond my convictions. I could not look at the man on a normal day, much less stand close enough to land a blow.

But my mother had it in her. Her threats for years of making him regret the day he was born were not in vain.

She smiled at me, but there was no joy in her eyes. Her face had been covered with blood, tears, and snot.

But she spoke after some time of us standing there in perpetual silence.

"It was too much, you know." Her words were cold and matter-of-fact. "He just kept beating me, and for years, I thought it was okay. I thought I deserved it."

I watched her speak, as if finally facing the truth before her. My heart thumped in my ear as the memories of the last 15 years played on repeat like a late-night sitcom they forgot to turn off. I stood and listened because even if I never saw her again, she deserved at least one moment where she was the star.

"I thought he would stop. Thought if I were the perfect wife, he would love me enough not to hurt me." She paused to soak in the words or find just the right ones. "But he didn't, and I couldn't love him enough to make him love me."

I wanted to hug her and tell her it would be alright. Tell her he deserved it and so much more. I wanted to tell her she was a good wife, even if that meant she was a neglectful mother.

But I said nothing. I did not want to speak anymore in this household. I had packed my bags for a reason.

"I'm sorry," her voice quivered as she tried to wrap her robe around herself. "I know this is my fault, but now it's my doing."

"You leave and find a better place. Somewhere, we can't find you. You deserve that; if nothing else, you deserve that."

Her words caught me off guard. It was the most she had spoken to me in the last five years. My heart did not mourn her ragged face. But a small part of me wanted to hug her and remind her of when we loved each other.

My mother's cold smile returned to me, and I knew that was my answer. There was nothing left for me.

For a moment, I wanted her to ask me to stay. I wanted her to promise me our family could heal. Swallowing down the need for forgiveness I had not yet learned to attain, I picked up my bags and left.

What happened after my leaving was a mystery to me. Though, I hoped she was brave enough for the consequences of ending a life.

I know I had to learn what it meant to leave seven stabs in another person and drug someone else into believing they had finally freed themselves.

But that is a different story, one I will die with.

Saheem and The Trip to Nowhere

A Short Story by Jona Nightingale

Saheem held his binder to his chest and ran, he was going to be late for school, again.

It was the third time this month he had been late. But this time it was not his fault, he had a perfect reason for being late.

He had found his way walking through a black lagoon on the world of Istila searching for treasure and a new future. Hoping, his treasure hunting could afford him top surgery and a move across the country for college.

Saheem doubted his guardians would allow it, but he was almost 18 now and in two months, the state would consider him adult enough to vote and get a better body. One that didn't haunt him so fiercely every waking moment.

But he didn't have time to think about the little black book, treasures, or the promises it held. He was going to have to catch the next bus and that would mean he had missed his favorite class, first period with Miss Davis.

He loved the way her classroom made him feel, so warm and cozy. Miss Davis taught Advanced Physics, Saheem wasn't sure why seniors needed so much physics in their lives, but he had run out of classes to take in his last semester of school.

The bus came while Saheem was thinking of the joke Miss Davis recently told in class. But looking to greet the bus driver's eyes was enough to make Saheem frown. Mr. Fraser was not a mean man, but he had a way of being so arrogant in his ignorance, that you only had to look at him to have a bad day.

Saheem boarded the bus and looked away from the driver. But he still heard it, that low chuckle and a whistle. It made his skin crawl.

I take it back, he's just another creeper, he thought to himself. *Only creepers and pedophiles hit on teenagers.* It was a fact.

He made his way to the back of the bus and placed his bag in his lap. That's when he saw it, he had forgotten to bind his chest properly and now a pair of obvious breasts stared back at him.

If there was any way for the world to swallow him up, he begged for it to be now. But the world did not respond, and then Saheem had a thought.

There was only one way to leave this horrible situation. But it would be such a drastic measure for his embarrassment.

He reached in his bag for the black book that granted his dreams and nightmares. *I really shouldn't do this,* he thought to himself, but he had already started writing.

Anywhere, but here.

Saheem should have remembered all the lessons he learned while traveling with the black book. The book had a terrible sense of humor and direction unless you directly asked for a specific location. You would end up where the book had in mind. And normally that was never a place you wanted to be.

Saheem had once written about a mountain of treasure. The book had thrown him into a dragon's lair. Saheem had never been so terrified in all his life, he had learned the hard way that the book was not exactly his friend.

It was more like a cruel mentor. The book had been passed down in his family and when his parents died, he inherited it along with a house he could no longer call home.

His new guardians had moved him to live with them, but it was more like he was being monitored. He lived in the attic like some sort of forsaken orphan and only ventured out of the house to go to school and the library.

Saheem preferred to go to the library and then straight to the hut in the woods where he spent all his free time. There he had made his second trip with the little black book. He wanted to explore a jungle, and so the little book took him to a jungle that should not have existed.

The creature grew fangs and moved with the shadows. Saheem would have died had it not been for help from some of the native inhabitants of the forest. But soon he knew that they only rescued him because he had been prophesied to become a sacrifice to their god.

A blade sunk into his chest, and then he was back in his bed. His clothes were covered in blood and sweat, but when he checked his chest, there was nothing. Not even a scar.

Saheem did not travel with the book for a long time after that, he was too scared to do so. The book had taken him to the farthest corners of the 100 worlds and killed him. With each death, Saheem had found far fewer treasures than he had hoped.

The jewels he had tried to snatch from the dragon's lair were ripped from his pockets. Gold coins were often snatched away by some crook or thief.

But Saheem was determined to just have enough treasure to change his life. He had to leave this horrible city that only made him feel small and frightened when he walked the street.

He lived in an attic, so any place would have been better than this house.

And yet he ended up nowhere.

The book had taken Saheem to the dark corners of the universe, where only rocks existed. He tried not to think about how he was still breathing, or if any planet near him had a source of water.

He had learned to always be prepared. So in his bag, had been two sets of lunch, a water bottle, a first aid kit, a flashlight, a jacket, and a knife. He knew he couldn't carry the knife to school, so he often stashed it in a bush near his school.

There were too many rocks around him for much light to shine through the debris. Instantly Saheem knew two things; one he was in an asteroid belt and two, there was some sort of treasure nearby.

He hoped it would be some type of mineral that he could bring back with him. This would be the first time finding a mineral, but he had read enough space stories to know that some parts of asteroids contained minerals formed over time. Saheem just had to find it and hoped that no space monsters were lurking in the shadows waiting to eat him.

It was always thoughts like these that led him into trouble or said trouble to him. He had yet to figure out that the little black book could read his mind, and it had a twisted sense of humor and adventure.

Sure it had wanted Saheem to find enough treasure to leave that horrible place he called home, but it also wanted to go to more places. So it might have orchestrated an unfortunate incident or two on these little adventures.

Truthfully, it was doing it for Saheem. It needed him to become an adventurer. To wished to explore the unknown, and right now he was a bit weak.

Obviously, he had been stronger after dying a few times, but death tends to do that to you.

So with each death, Saheem became more determined to find a way to survive. He was also braver in school now and at home. Surely, it would pay off eventually.

The book just had to keep feeding Saheem experiences where he became a stronger person, and then it would take him to the places where the treasure was guaranteed rather than just a training exercise.

The little black book smiled to itself, as if a book could smile at all. It wrinkled its pages and shook as it laughed.

If only Saheem had heard the laughter, then he would have known something terrible was about to happen to him.

A shiver ran down his spine as he tried not to think about how he was breathing in space, or what monster would he face this time.

He reached for his knife and tried to shuffle himself forward. Most people did not know how to move in a zero-gravity environment, and that included Saheem. He flapped his arms and legs to gain some momentum but not much happened.

He was stuck, but not for long, as a giant rock moved towards him.

Now was the time for action, he reached out with all his might and shimmied his body towards the rock. Saheem was just barely able to stab his knife into the surface of the rock. Smiling to himself, he was glad he remembered to take the knife from the trunk his parents had left him.

It was unlike any knife he had known before, its blade extended in times of crisis and retracted to form a weapon small enough to fit in his back pocket if he needed it. The handle contained a yellow jewel that sparkled in the moonlight to act as a torch.

A buzzing sound came from the jewel, as it was about to ignite. Saheem should have paid attention to this new development, but he was too busy trying to orientate himself to which direction was up and which was down.

So far it had been a tiresome ordeal, *I should work out more if I'm going to keep treasure hunting.*

The thought was more of a passing comment, but he knew it was true. All his adventures had taught him three things; one, he was far too weak, two, he needed to plan for hostile environments, and three, there was something deeper to this than he understood.

It did not escape him how he was unable to bring home any treasures, or the fact that each adventure was more dangerous than the last. It was as if the book was testing him, just to see if he would break.

As Saheem figured out how to retrieve the knife that had become a sword, he stood upright on the rock and began to walk about exploring. His backpack also contained a notebook for his observations. But he didn't want to take the book out and lose it in space. He knew his backpack would return to him once he returned home, but he wasn't so sure about the contents.

Sometimes things went missing and other times, he would find a leaf or a branch in his backpack. He once had a backpack filled with sand on his journey back from the desert.

He had begun to wonder if his bag was special, like the knife or the little black book, but it wasn't. Saheem had bought it before the school year began. And yet it returned to him every time it got lost along the way.

It had to be magical, but Saheem wasn't sure how. That was the question that rumbled on the edge of his mind as he explored the rock.

There was a shallow depression in the rock that held what could first be confused as water, but it was simply a gas. It shimmered in the light, glowing softly. Saheem wanted to touch it, to feel its texture, but he knew better than that.

Curiosity was the one thing that would have to be used sparingly on these adventures. Not much good came from being curious about his surroundings.

Once, when Saheem had been quite curious about the plants and animals that grew in the forest on his third trip, he walked right into a trap. For days, he hung upside down, waiting for someone to rescue him from the error of his ways. In time, he learned that curiosity was only helpful if the area was safe to explore.

More often than not, he had to be extremely careful. But Saheem forgot this while he watched the pool of vapor flowing like water in the forest. He didn't seem to notice how the asteroids near him began to shake and change in size.

Even if he had been scanning the area, nothing could make a sound in space. In a vacuum, there was no noise. No indicator of impending doom, just the natural ability and will to survive.

Saheem felt the urge to turn around just when the final rock connected to the golem. It stood 12 feet tall as it moved through the asteroid belt, jumping from one surface to the other.

For a moment, Saheem stood there, frozen in fear as all the neurons in his body told him to move. The heat from the knife in his hand jolted him awake from his statue-like state, and he turned and ran.

The golem was bigger and faster than him, closing the distance in seconds. A solid hand dropped from the sky and knocked Saheem out of the way.

It wasn't the golem that had hit him. It was a small hand that had nothing connected to it. Saheem landed on what felt like clouds. He was sure he had landed on rocks, but around him were soft patches of earth.

The small hand faced off the golem. Saheem felt like this amazing moment was the perfect time to whip out his notebook to sketch the image before him. But logic told him differently. The golem looked at the hand and yelled. At least, that's what it would have sounded like if Saheem could hear the sound.

The golem lunged forward, ignoring the hand and heading straight for Saheem. He tried to stand to his feet, but the dirt was too soft and he kept losing his balance.

What a moment to be proven as a klutz, Saheem thought. *Perfect for taking out the weaker one first.*

The hand rearranged its trajectory and smashed into the side of the golem's head. The momentum sent the golem spiraling back, and it tried to catch its balance. It roared its silence warning again while sending a rock sailing at the hand that tried to stop him from catching its prey.

Saheem was almost free from the soft dirt now, he wouldn't call it quicksand, because he wasn't being swallowed alive. But it was enough of a problem to make him wish he had a hook of some sort to give him leverage while he dragged himself to solid ground.

If he had been thinking outside the box, he would have remembered he wasn't grounded in space. With a little push in the opposite direction, he could have run away from the fight.

When the hand came out of the tussle victorious, Saheem was beginning to grow concerned. Why had the hand helped him in the first place? Was it to connect to the rest of its body? Perhaps the hand was all there was to this species, and then it hit him.

The hand launched itself towards Saheem with the golem's core in its palm. For a moment Saheem thought the hand rejoiced, but that would have been too far absurd to even imagine. Luckily, the hand didn't seem dangerous now, it was not here to hurt him. It could have been a guardian.

Occasionally something like a guardian or protector would show up on certain worlds. It was almost as if they were waiting for him to appear. They hardly ever spoke his language and if they did, most did not appreciate the way he looked or dressed.

Saheem's hair was shoulder-length held back from his face by a small hair tie, he had locked it in the past few years due to just how fast it grew. With this style, he could cut the ends easily. Once every three months, he would trim his hair and remind himself that soon his face wouldn't look so feminine all the time.

But that all depended on his ability to use the little black book to find the treasures that he sought. So far he had not been able to bring back any treasure. At first, he had thought it was because he was a klutz, and while that statement had some truth to it. Saheem often thought of how he would convert the treasure to money.

Who would actually trust him enough to buy the goods without alerting the authorities? There were very little adults he trusted, and even less so himself.

Perhaps all he needed to do was hold on for two more months, when he could claim the inheritance he knew his parents left for him. The one his relatives didn't know about and would never know about if he did it right.

But Saheem was getting tired of looking in the mirror each day and hating his reflection. He wanted the changes to happen now, not in ten years, when he had more responsibilities than he knew what to do with.

He frowned as he watched the hand approach him, it did not seem to hold any malicious intentions. But how could he tell a good had from a bad one?

Saheem hated thinking about the creature as a hand, the jokes that came to his mind made his lips twitch with a smirk. He just hoped his experiences up to now would come in handy for later.

The hand offered the core to Saheem without hesitation. It dropped it at his feet and creeped away using its fingers as if they were two little legs. What a moment of disbelief.

If someone had asked Saheem what he thought today would have been like, he was not likely to say, "following after a purple hand with a golem's core in my bag."

He would have talked about how he hated chemistry class because the teacher seemed out to get him, or why he stayed away from the cafeteria at lunchtime.

He would not have told you about learning to walk in space and being hungry but not sure how much time has passed.

Saheem doubted he would have told anyone about the way the hand led him to an old discarded station on the largest asteroid he had ever seen.

But there he stood at a gate letting lasers scan him as he entered into the base, still confused on why he followed the hand without even thinking.

Once his brain started questioning one thing, it questioned everything. How was he now more unaware of his breathing? Could he eat here? When was the last time he ate? What would he find beyond the gate?

As questions plagued his mind, Saheem realized he could feel the breeze for the first time since he got on the bus. Inside the gate looked like an entire town filled with lively colors, pink rooftops and markets that busied with hands moving to and fro. It was a sight to see.

Hands of every different shapes and sizes busied themselves as if they were people. They were furry hands with dark and slick fur, scaly hands that left a trail of water in its passing, and so many others.

A nation of things that come in handy.

Saheem couldn't help the thought and smiled to himself. But he still couldn't get over the warm breeze that greeted his face. It smelled like raw herbs and spices, with a hint of stench from the gutter.

Other than the bustling of the hands moving about, the town was silent. No one spoke, except is fast movements of their fingers as if they were using a sign language of their own.

Of course a town made up of only hands would us sign language, it was common sense. And yet so intriguing. But not all hands had five fingers, some only had one or two, Saheem wondered to himself how did they speak.

That's when it occurred to him there must be different types of communication here. Instead of only signing, there must be some sort of tapping language that only some hands could speak. But as he continues to walk through the city, he saw there weren't only hands here. What could only be considered as a claw hopped pass him in a hurry as if it were running.

Saheem was fascinated and reached for his notebook to write down what he saw. He wanted to capture the structures and creatures that went about their daily lives around him.

He took his time to roughly sketch market and the different types of hands he saw. It wasn't until his pencil fell that he realize the concept of gravity had been replicated in this town.

It didn't make logical sense, but he had learned a long time ago to remove the bias of earth conversations. Making it easier to move pass his own thoughts, he drew even faster. He wanted to capture all the small details before it left his vision.

Saheem felt the urge to sit and draw, but then he remembered that he was supposed to be following the hand. It was larger some of the other hands around. It came to his waist, and Saheem was particularly taller than most of his peers.

His parents had been on the shorter side, but they had assured him that he got his height from his grandparents. Of course, it had been come a huge topic in the family. His parents were no taller than 5"3' and here he was almost 6 feet tall.

He looked more like he belonged to his guardians with his height, than his own little family of warmth and comfort. Saheem tried not to think about it as he hurried his steps to catch up with the hand.

It had made its way a few yards away before it turned around and realized its guest of honor was not following closely behind as she had instructed. She had made sure to use the simplest language she knew, since it seemed like a lower life form.

But it had still failed to understand the honor it had been granted. So she gave it the golem's core to hold on to and led the way to the town they had made in the last few hundred years.

She could sense its confusion, but none the less, she had a mission to accomplish. And nothing was going to stand in her way, not even this odd shaped life form. Truthfully it looked like a lesser form of her master. It had the same head and body, but she couldn't be too sure about it.

It had been a while since she saw her master whole as the gods. Most main bodies were locked away for years to undergo the evolutionary process of this solar system. Without it, they would truly die out in time.

This solar system only created a set number of beings as if it had an expiration date or presented the results of an experiment. If they had not found a way to preserve their life, they would have spent the rest of their existence devolving into the nothingness of time and space.

She waited patiently for the life form to follow her. It looked like an altered version of her existence had she not chosen self-evolution over a condemned fate. It tittered after her, dodging other races and using its upper region to produce noise. She was sure that the creature was somehow trying to communicate with them and failing tragically.

The creature caught up to her rather quickly and once again made noises as if she could understand it. But what was more interesting to her was the small objects it carried. She had seen drawings like this once a long time ago when it was her mission to explore an extinct race of inventors and researchers for their people.

They had walls covered with similar writings and drawings in each room. It seemed they have round out of space in their systems to record their discoveries, so they took to the walls. It was a marvel to see and one she would never forget.

Saheem approached the hand with caution, he could tell that it had waited for him. But how did it know to wait for him? Could it see him?

As far as he could tell, he had not seen any eyes on the creatures as they walked past each other and, yet, they never bumped into each other. They could even pick up things with precision.

He became even more curious the more he watched them. This trip had been the most time he had ever had to observe his surroundings. He was usually fighting for his life or running away from danger.

Typically, he would wake up the next day and wonder if it had been a dream or a real adventure. Then he would look at his clothes and immediately he could tell which was which. When he went on an adventure, his clothes was would usually have holes and tears in them. Sometimes bits of pieces would be covered in blood.

Each time he stepped into a new world, his body would be placed in optimal condition for his survival. Perhaps that's why he wanted to start working out more, he was far too weak for these bizarre worlds he found himself in at times.

Saheem's clothes were fine for now, it seems that while he was in space a force field had formed around him. Even when he had rolled around in the soft dirt, he had been fine.

But now bits of dust had begun to stick to the hem of his jeans. At first, he wasn't bothered by it, now those bits of dust were starting to turn his jeans black at the hem. It almost seemed like they were eroding away the bits and pieces of his clothes.

It was a good thing he packed other clothes in his bag, just in case these were ruined.

He tried not to think about how the pathway continued to darken and narrowed as they moved towards their location. Saheem could feel the warmth of the jewel from the knife and knew that it sensed his nervousness. His heart rate skyrocketed as the floor fell out from under his feet.

Saheem did not have time to scream as he was plunged into darkness. Of course, he tried to scream, to shout, to make any sound from his mouth, but he soon found out that not one word could leave him.

He had lost his ability to speak as he fell into the great void. He tried to flail around and hold on to something, but he just kept falling without moving from the same spot. He could move neither left nor right, and the fright of falling had not worn off in the last few moments as he fell.

Saheem screamed, but nothing came out except for puffs of white smoke.

There was no end in sight, and the darkness prevented him from seeing his surroundings. But he could still make out the parts of his body, it was what lay beyond that point which frustrated him. All around him, a coldness had started to sip into his bones.

The armor that had surrounded in space was no more of a help than it was now for falling. Well, at least gravity was still playing its part in his grand plan of falling to his death. There has to always be a silver lining. His voiceless screams came out as white thick clouds that floated just above his head. He flung his arm up and tried to grab it with all his might.

But it hit against something hard and metal with a thwang sound that vibrated through his body. Clouds were not usually hard or made of metal; clouds were soft and malleable with a bit of air current and heat added to them.

He swore to himself, that if he could just find a way to stop falling, then he would definitely leave this horrible place of hands and feet.

Saheem had a thought about how to escape this horrible predicament and once he did, he would find the hand that led him there and give it a proper scolding.

If Saheem was in a better mood, he would have chuckled to himself at how silly this had all become, but alas, he was not. Then he had a thought, the clouds followed him as he fell and if he had enough of them together, he could perhaps float as well.

The surrounding air created a vacuum, bringing the clouds down with him as he went. This was going to be a problem, if he could only make himself enough clouds, then he would be able to use it.

He started to scream with all his might, clouds lunged from his mouth into the surrounding air. Before long, there was a large enough cloud to hold him and his bag without falling apart. Testing the sturdiness of the cloud, he tried to hit it a bit gentler this time.

It felt like the railing on his headboard, the metal thwang gave off the same sound as he hit it a second time to reassure himself of the sturdiness of the cloud. He took a deep breath in and hauled himself up onto the cloud.

Instantly, he noticed two things about the cloud that he had created; one, it was a lot softer than he could have imagined and two, he was far too comfortable laying down on it.

It almost felt like a bed.

What Saheem didn't know was that he had never actually fallen down into darkness in the first place, or if he had simply fallen asleep. He had never gotten on the bus or missed first period. The hand and the golem had been a part of his imagination.

He was dreaming. A nightmare, but it was still a dream.

By the time he realized that cloud was the bed, the sun was beginning to rise over the horizon. A thought came to him as he slowly awoke, *Perhaps hands and feet only came in one form.*

His room was the way he had left it before falling asleep last night, pieces of paper laid on the floor, and a cup of, once piping hot, tea sat on his desk.

The only thing that were out of place were the black book and a round object that vaguely looked like the golem's core he had been given.

It didn't make sense and for the first time in a long time, Saheem decided not to question the logic behind what happen.

As he went to the bathroom, rubbing the dream from his eyes, he made sure to pick up his binder and put it on. It might have been a dream, but he had no intention of letting the same thing happen again.

This time when he went on an adventure, he would be ready, binder on and little book ready to go to places beyond his imagination. At the very least it would be better than anywhere but here. Not nowhere but a place with a treasure waiting for him.

He now knew what he would become, a treasure hunter. An explorer.

Perhaps, after the two months were up and he could go out in the world again as himself. Then he would take on the entire universe and find out just what his parents really did for a living. It was time for an adventure of a lifetime, just hopefully he would be prepared.

Today would be the first day of building his strength to explore. Just right after breakfast.

He had it coming

A Short Story by Jona Nightingale

I have never thought of myself as a killer.

Blood made me queasy, and I even failed college biology because I wouldn't dissect the frog for the assignment. I clearly remember running from the lab to go empty my guts. I didn't make it to the bathroom or trashcan in time.

Not only that, but I was shunned from labs for an entire semester and could only do theoretical projects, which I also failed.

So when the neighbor came over to pull me off my brother's corpse, I cried, telling them it wasn't me.

I could have never done something like that. Even now, my body is shaking at the thought of whichever monster could have lured me there to frame me.

My brother was a good person; he was occasionally mean and would hit me. But isn't that what all families are like?

No? Well, you must have had a different kind of family then. In my household, there were bruises on everyone. Yes, even my doctor knew about it, but what could they do? None of them were willing to put their career on the line to make the pain stop. So we learned to live with it.

As I said, I couldn't have done it. Oh, these scratches? Those must have come from our fight the night before. He tried to stop me from leaving the house, but I had a date for the first time in years.

You can't imagine how excited I was to have one of my old friends back in town. I hadn't seen Samantha in years, and she even asked me on a date. So, I said yes.

But my brother was against it when I finally told him where I was going. He threatened to use the branding tool our dad used to punish us when he was still alive.

Oh? That's not in your report; that's weird. Didn't the doctor tell you how I got the scars on my hands and feet?

It's a fascinating story; when our mom heard our screams for the first time, she would turn away. I thought she was a cold woman until I saw her scars. She was just like us. "One of the herd." That's what my father used to say about being the good shepherd for our family.

Forgive me; I tend to ramble when I talk. No, I did not have any trauma from my childhood.

Believe me, detective, I want to help you catch the criminal as much as anyone. My poor brother was stabbed to death.

No, I don't usually cry over things like death. My mother taught us that when she killed our dad.

Oh? That's not what your investigation says. No worries, this town has its own way of caring for those who harm us. You should ask your supervisor about the case, they'll tell you that he committed suicide, but it was our mom that pushed him off that bridge.

She let us watch her do it. You would never believe what she said afterward. "The fucker had it coming."

Oh, sorry. I am rambling again.

No, I definitely didn't do it. I could not even stand the sight of my own blood flowing down the sink on my ritual cuttings. There is no way I could have done something like that.

What? Are ritual cuttings, not a thing? Impossible; we all did them in my family. Next, you will tell me you did not get buried when you misbehaved.

Detective, you should focus more on finding my brother's killer instead of talking ill about my family. They were all good people.

No, I do not know anything about the bodies in my backyard. How could I? I was not allowed in the backyard except for punishment.

You are beginning to insult my good nature; I have done nothing but answer your questions with honest replies.

Thank you for believing me, detective. I am an honest person. Do you perhaps have a place where I can shower?

They only gave me a blanket when they ushered me into the interrogation room, and I wanted to wash all the dirt off me before it ruined my skirt.

It looks a bit red, but I think that's from kneeling over the corpse for so long. I couldn't bring myself to look away.

Not saying I like blood at all, but my mother would have said the same thing as she did when my father died.

"He had it coming."

Maybe she was a cold woman, after all.

No, I don't remember where I put any of the knives.

Is that all, detective? Good. I was starting to grow suspicious that you believed I was a monster. I'm glad I can go back home now and rest.

Thank you, have a good night as well.

The End

Family Dinner by Jona Nightingale

Also by Jona Nightingale

The Fates
The Poison of Fate

Standalone
Family Dinner
Screaming in the Forest

Watch for more at www.jonanightingale.com.

About the Author

Jona Nightingale (they/he) is a Jamaican-born, an openly queer trans writer and poet living in the Northeast US. They believe in power of representation, reading for chaos, and celebrating culture and creativity with whimsy. If you see them in a cafe or bookstore, know that they are up plotting something devious and strange.

When Jona isn't writing, you can find him talking with his chickens, sharing stories with his bestie, or drinking a nice cup of hot tea. You can follow them for more book and writing updates on BlueSky @jonanightingale.bsky.social or TikTok and Instagram @jonathenightingale.

Read more at www.jonanightingale.com.